Robert Louis Stevenson's

DR. JEKYLL AND MR. HYDE

Retold by Samantha Lee

General Editor: John Halkin

BARRON'S

New York

Also available in the
Fleshcreeper series

THE VAMPYRE
BLOOD FROM THE MUMMY'S TOMB
FANGS OF THE WEREWOLF
FRANKENSTEIN

First edition for the United States and the Philippines
published 1988 by Barron's Educational Series, Inc.

First published 1987 by Hutchinson Children's Books, an
imprint of Century Hutchinson Ltd, London, England.

All inquiries should be addressed to:
Barron's Educational Series, Inc.
250 Wireless Boulevard
Hauppauge, New York 11788

Library of Congress Catalog Card No. 88-16599

International Standard Book No. 0-8120-4072-4

Library of Congress Cataloging-in-Publication Data
Lee, Samantha.
    Robert Louis Stevenson's Dr. Jekyll and Mr. Hyde /
retold by Samantha Lee : general editor, John Halkin.
    p. cm.—(Fleshcreepers)
    Summary: A retelling of the tale about the scientist who
drinks a potion that he has created and becomes a murderous
monster.
    ISBN 0-8120-4072-4
    [1. Horror stories.] I. Stevenson, Robert Louis,
1850-1894.
Strange case of Dr. Jekyll and Mr. Hyde. II. Halkin, John, ill.
III. Title. IV. Title: Dr. Jekyll and Mr. Hyde. V. Series.
PZ7.L514855Ro 1988
[Fic]—dc19   88-16599
                                                        CIP
PRINTED IN THE UNITED STATES OF AMERICA   AC
890 5500 987654321

About this Book

Some fictional characters become so famous that their names are now part of the English language. Jekyll and Hyde are two of them—no, I should say *one* of them.

Tales of ghosts, ghoulies and vampires have always been popular, but when Robert Louis Stevenson sat down in 1886 to write *The Strange Case of Dr. Jekyll and Mr. Hyde* he looked for his fleshcreeping horror into the depths of the human soul itself. What he found there has terrified his readers ever since.

At that time, Stevenson was already well known as the successful author of *Treasure Island* and the creator of Long John Silver, but in this new story he entered a more frightening world. The virtuous Dr. Jekyll treating his patients day and night while devoting his spare time to medical research in his own laboratory —well, any of Stevenson's readers would have recognized *that* character from real life. But experiments can lead along strange paths. When Dr. Jekyll begins to dabble in the problems of human good and evil he little realizes what end is in store for him.

People often say that there is good and bad in everyone. Such people have never met Edward Hyde, the embodiment of pure evil who is released on the world not merely once but again . . . and again . . . terrorizing the London streets.

John Halkin

But first on earth, as vampires sent,
Thy corse shall from the tomb be rent,
Then ghastly haunt thy native place
And suck the blood of all thy race.
                    Lord Byron, *The Giaour*

ONE

Sebastopol Street was empty.

Except for the child.

And the dark figure watching.

The figure stood in a doorway. A silent shadow. Gray. Menacing. Swathed from head to toe in an oversized opera cloak.

The mist of the London evening twirled and eddied around the figure until its indistinct outline misted and blurred, became a shadow within a shadow.

A magician's illusion.

Now you see it, now you don't.

Midway down the cobbled street, the Dog and Duck Tavern beckoned like a bright oasis through the murk. Light beamed invitingly from its windows. The sound of the tinny piano, overlaid now and then by a screech of raucous laughter, filtered out into the November night.

The child, a girl of about five years old, sat on the pavement outside the pub, her bare feet dangling in the gutter. The gaslight spilling from the inn haloed her golden curls, giving her the aspect of a fallen angel.

Closer to, the reality was less romantic.

Matted blonde hair tumbled around her grimy face and fell over her soiled pinafore which, together with a thin dress, was all that protected her from the chill of the autumn air. Her legs were mottled with bruises and her fingernails bitten to the quick. She chewed one reflectively, worrying at a hangnail with small, uneven teeth.

3

Her nose began to run. She wiped it with the back of her hand and began to snivel quietly. It was almost an hour since her mother had gone into the pub and the child wished she would hurry up. She was cold; and hungry; and tired out.

At the far end of the street, the figure began to move. It darted from one doorway to the next, cloak fluttering like the wings of a vampire bat.

The child caught the movement out of the corner of her eye and swivelled her head sharply as her heart gave a sudden leap of apprehension.

But there was nothing.

Only the fog, darkening the dusk over the blank face of the buildings.

She turned her attention back to the contents of the gutter.

And behind her the figure moved closer, avoiding the pools of light under the gaslamps.

It reached the pub and hunkered down, a huge, misshapen spider crouched under the protective overhang of the doorsills.

Then, slowly, with crablike motion, it began to sidle sideways towards the child.

An empty matchbox floated by in the stagnant stream beneath the little girl's feet. She bent to pick it up, wiping away the corpse of a crumpled leaf that clung to one side.

The voice whispered in her ear. Silky. Smooth as a striking snake.

"Hello, my pretty," said the voice. "And what are you doing, all alone?"

Daisy simpered.

Often, when she had been waiting for her mother, some kind person had taken pity on her and given her a cake or a sweetmeat. Once an old gentleman with white hair had given her a whole penny, and then gone into the Dog and Duck and dragged her mother out and told her to "take the child home to its bed."

She had stared and stared at that bright penny, imagining all the things she might buy with it the next day.

But when the old man had gone on his grumbling way, her mother had snatched it and gone back into the pub to spend it, giving her a smack round the head when she protested.

So it hadn't been so lucky after all.

Still, you never knew.

Putting on her most sugary smile, she turned her head in the direction of the voice.

The eyes that leered out at her from under the hood had a strange, longing look. Her instincts flared, warning her that this was no kindly stranger.

This was something altogether different . . .

Something dangerous . . . and infinitely nasty.

She opened her mouth to cry out.

But before she could suck enough air into her narrow lungs for a good yell, a hand clamped across her face: a broad, spatulate hand, brown and corded and immensely strong. Black hairs sprouted from the back of it. They tickled her nostrils, making her want to sneeze.

And then another hand curled round her waist, holding her tight, lifting her up and away from the gutter, up past the folds of the opera cape, up towards the dreadful eyes and even more dreadful face that lurked beneath the velvet hood.

Her heart began to flutter in her chest. Her frail limbs thrashed feebly as she tried to wriggle free.

5

But still the arm raised her slowly, firmly, closer to the face.

She didn't want to see it.

Didn't want to look.

She closed her eyes tight.

And then the lifting stopped.

She opened her eyes. And the face was there. Next to hers. She couldn't get away from it.

It was hardly a human face at all.

Thick hair grew low on the forehead, a thin line of swarthy skin showing between the scalp and the overgrown eyebrows. The feverish eyes stared out at her, hypnotizing her as a cobra might mesmerize a rabbit.

The nose was broad and flat with dilated nostrils.

All the better to smell you with, my dear.

The mouth was wide too, with full lips drawn back over strong white teeth. The incisors were pointed like a jackal's and the breath was a dog's breath, panting in the loll-tongued mouth. Not evil smelling but carrying on it the taint of something bestial. It warmed and cooled her face as the figure breathed in and out. And as she watched, her eyes dilated in terror, a small spittle of saliva formed in the corner of the lips and dribbled down the chin.

"Don't be afraid, little girl," said the voice, "nobody's going to hurt you."

But the tone and the eyes said something different, so she struggled frantically as the strong arms began to wrap her in the all-enveloping shroud of the opera cloak.

A sudden bellow of laughter erupted from the pub and then a woman's voice calling out in a harsh cockney accent.

"'Ere. What are you doing with my Daisy?"

The arms loosed their hold as the figure whirled towards the doorway.

"What is it, Dolly?"

A well-built man in his late twenties, slightly the worse for drink, stumbled from the pub to join the woman.

"This blighter's got hold of my Daisy," she said belligerently. "Put 'er down, you dirty old man, or I'll belt you one."

The figure backed away, the woman following. With one hand she scrabbled for the face while with the other she tried to tweak the child away. Her raking fingernails caught the side of the hood, wrenching it back and exposing the creature's head.

The woman stopped dead in her tracks.

The man behind her drew a sharp, audible intake of breath.

"My God," he said weakly. "What is it?"

The thing—you could scarcely call it a man—snarled low in its throat and threw the couple a look that froze the marrow in their bones. Then it hurled the child away, cracking her head against the pub wall before she slid, like a rag doll, to the pavement. Dragging the hood back over its head, the figure took off down the street.

As though awakened from a collective nightmare, the woman began to scream and the man to shout.

The doors and windows were flung wide as the occupants of the Dog and Duck—always eager to applaud a domestic battle—spewed out on to the road to get a better view of the anticipated fight.

Instead they found Dolly Coates cradling the crumpled figure of her daughter in her arms and Tom Tompkins, her current beau, lurching up Sebastopol Street in pursuit of a hooded shape.

TWO

"He's killed her," screamed Dolly. "He's made mince-meat of my Daisy."

"Come on, lads," roared Tom over his shoulder. "Give us a hand here. Don't let the bum get away."

Several of the more sober citizens made to follow Tom. However, even the more sober citizens were not *very* sober, and those that were stopped to down their ale before giving chase. They knew that if they didn't someone else would have drunk it for them before they got back.

So all in all, what with the speed at which he traveled and the tardiness of his pursuers, the figure would have got clean away had he not rounded the corner into Alma Crescent and run smack into the arms of young Richard Enfield.

Enfield was on his way home from a party and in a particularly pleasant frame of mind when the cloaked figure hurtled round the corner with head bent and caught him full in the chest, knocking the breath from his body. So great was the impact that the runaway bounced back from the taller man like a ricocheting bullet, tripped over a loose flagstone and sprawled in a heap on the ground.

"I say, old man," said Enfield, bending to assist the prostrate figure. "I do beg your pardon."

But instead of taking his proffered hand as Enfield expected, the creature lunged at him and sank its teeth into his palm.

Enfield cried out in surprise and pain. But he was an enterprising young man, well-versed in the arts of self-defense. Bunching his free hand into a fist, he caught his antagonist squarely on the side of the head, causing him to grunt and release his hold.

Enfield began to massage his bleeding hand.

"What in blue blazes did you do that for?" he protested angrily, but the dazed figure was already scrambling up.

From the direction of Sebastopol Street came the sounds of running feet and raised voices.

"Oh no you don't," said Enfield, and he grabbed the figure by the scruff of the neck as it darted by.

The young cavalry officer was tall and exceptionally well-built, but he found the fugitive, who barely reached his shoulder, to be amazingly strong for his size. Also he fought with a fierceness born of desperation. So it was just as well that Tom Tompkins and six or seven of his cronies rounded the corner at this point and overwhelmed him by the sheer weight of numbers. They pinioned his arms to his sides and, with Enfield following behind, marched him back to the Dog and Duck.

A crowd had gathered round the injured child and a doctor had been summoned from one of the back rooms of the tavern to lend his inebriated skills to her revival.

Someone had brought a basin of water and a flannel and Dolly was bathing her daughter's head while the doctor—whose name was Marchmont—held a bottle of smelling salts under the little girl's nose.

"A concussion to the head, but from what I can see . . . hic . . . I . . . I do beg your pardon . . . no serious damage . . ." he rambled on. "She's had a . . . hic . . . nasty shock, of course."

"A shock," said Dolly. "I should say she has. If you'd

seed that bloke you'd've had a shock and all. Not normal
he wasn't. Looked like the very devil 'isself."

Tom Tompkins's voice rose above that of his lady
friend as he and his mates dragged the reluctant culprit
into the light.

"We got him, Dolly."

At the sound, Daisy opened her eyes.

She saw the figure.

She opened her eyes wider.

Then she opened her mouth . . . and screamed.

Her screams ripped through the curtain of mist,
echoing round the clefts and corners of Sebastopol Street
until even the hair on the neighborhood cats stood on
end.

"You fiend," screeched Dolly. "Look what you done
to my kid."

"Lucky that's all he done," shouted a female voice. "If
you hadn't of come out when you did, Dolly Coates,
he'd 'ave done a darn sight more."

"Let's see his face," snarled a man at the back.

"Yeah, let's see what he looks like."

"Pervert."

"Child beater."

"Dirty old man."

Hands reached out to grab the hood, plucking it away
from the figure's concealed head. It dropped back
falling in folds over the humped shoulders and round the
almost nonexistent neck.

A stunned hush fell over the crowd.

Daisy, all screamed out, whimpered in her mother's
arms and tried to make herself invisible.

No one spoke.

Even Enfield, who had seen some strange sights
during his time in the army, was at a loss for words. He

10

judged the fellow to be about the same age as himself. And yet there was an ancient, knowing quality about the eyes, that made him look much older.

Bullet head swivelling, the man searched around for a means of escape. But there was none. Fear clouded the knowing eyes, but there was cunning there too, and a kind of fierce pride at the effect he was having on the assembled throng. He chuckled, a wicked sound in his throat, and the inhabitants of Sebastopol Street, none of whom could be described as angels, shrank from him as they would from the Black Death.

Enfield was the first to recover himself.

"Who the devil are you, sir?" he demanded.

"You don't think he's going to give you his name, do you?" sneered a voice from the crowd.

"After what he done?"

"Some chance."

"No chance you mean."

"Afraid of the consequences."

"Afraid of the cops."

"Afraid his mother might find out."

"If he ever had a mother."

"I am not afraid." The man spoke with a hint of bravado and the voice, though flat and sibilant, was nonetheless an educated voice. The effect was curious. As though a monkey were talking the Queen's English. "My name is Hyde," he said, "Edward Hyde."

"Mr. . . . hic . . . Hyde, is it?" said the doctor, returning to the practicalities of life as he recovered his composure. "Well, Mr. . . . hic . . . Hyde . . . there is the matter of my . . . hic . . . pardon my . . . fee."

"Never mind your fee, you old penny pincher," cried someone in the crowd. "What about the kid?"

"Yeah, what about her?"

11

"And what about him?" yelled someone else. "What shall we do with him?"

Hate blazed up in them like a forest fire.

"Call the cops," called one.

"Yeah, turn him over to the law," shouted another.

"Naw. That's too good for him. Show him a bit of his own medicine."

"Give him a good hiding."

"Take him down the river and hold his head under the water."

"Hang him, I say."

"Who's gotta rope?"

The mob surged forward, fear, loathing and drink clouding their better judgment. It was clear they meant to hang the creature then and there.

Enfield raised his voice in protest.

"Come, come," he said. "What are we? Savages?"

The crowd subsided, rumbling.

"If you wish to make capital of this . . . misunderstanding," sneered Hyde. "I cannot, of course, stop you. I am one against many. However, a gentleman" (and here he looked at Enfield as though, heaven forbid, they might belong to the same club) ". . . a gentleman always tries to rectify his . . . mistakes. Let me go . . . and I can pay you for any . . . inconvenience suffered."

"How much?" said Dolly.

"Enough to have the child seen to by the best doctor in England. Twenty pounds."

"Twenty nicker?" Tom Tompkins whistled.

"I'll take it," said Dolly, sticking her hand out. "Now."

"You certainly will not," said Enfield. "This man should be dealt with by the full weight of the law."

"The law," snorted Tompkins. "He's a gent. The judge'll let him off."

"Yeah," said Dolly. "Mind your own business. Who asked you?" She turned back to Hyde. "Come on," she said, her daughter's welfare forgotten at the promise of such largesse, "put your money where your mouth is."

"Look at his clothes," protested Enfield, "the quality of the cloth. Clearly this is a man of means. Twenty pounds is nothing to him. If he is not to be prosecuted then at least make him pay a sufficient sum so that he will not forget this night in a hurry."

"How much?" Tompkins asked.

"A hundred pounds at least."

"A hundred pounds," sniggered Hyde. "Do you know what cretins like this would do with a hundred pounds? They'd drink themselves to death in a week."

"You have your nerve," said Dolly.

"A hundred pounds." Enfield was adamant. "Unless you'd like me to broadcast your part in this sorry affair all over town."

"A hundred pounds," said Tom, twisting Hyde's wrist up behind his back. "Unless you'd like your arm broke."

"You have me at a disadvantage," grimaced Hyde. "A hundred pounds it is."

The crowd began to cheer and clap each other on the back, rather as though they were all now in expectation of a fortune.

"Naturally," said Hyde, "I do not have the full amount on me."

Ribald laughter followed this announcement.

"Thought it was too good to be true," said Dolly. "How much have you got?"

"Ten pounds—no more."

"Ten pounds . . . a measly ten pounds?" Dolly sounded positively insulted. "Call the law."

"But if one of you . . . gentlemen," said Hyde, his voice heavily laced with sarcasm, "would care to accompany me home, I will give you a check for the remainder."

"I'll come," said Tom Tompkins.

"I take it you are the child's father?" said Enfield.

"He is like heck," said Dolly. "I'd better come meself. Just to make sure he don't do a runner with my money."

"You, madam," said Enfield, indicating the still shivering Daisy, "will get your daughter home to bed where she should have been many hours ago. I will accompany this gentleman—whatever his status" (he nodded in Tompkins's direction) "—and undertake to collect the check on your behalf."

"Oh yeah?" said Dolly. "And how do I know *you* won't do a runner with my money?"

Enfield produced his card and handed it to her.

"I'm afraid," he said, "you'll just have to take my word for that."

* * *

They bound Hyde's hands behind his back and looped a noose around his neck, and in this way (Enfield holding the rope like a man walking his dog) the three men proceeded through the maze of back streets and winding walkways that made up the Soho district of London.

The fog had come down in earnest now, so that, after a few minutes, Enfield totally lost his sense of direction.

The captive, however, evidently had no such problem. Even though they kept well away from the main thoroughfares so as not to attract attention, he appeared to know exactly where he was going. Stopping occasionally to sniff the night air like an animal following his nose, he led them on until half an hour later they drew up before a heavily fortified door in a narrow lane.

They untied his hands.

Hyde produced a heavy iron key from the folds of his cloak and let himself in.

Minutes later, when Enfield and Tompkins were just beginning to fear that they might have been duped, he reappeared carrying a check drawn on Coutts Bank.

Enfield scanned the signature and looked up sharply at Hyde.

His voice, when he spoke, was deadly cold.

"How do you know this gentleman?" he enquired.

"I know him as I know myself," smirked Hyde. "He is closer to me than anyone else in the world."

Enfield looked at the dissipated and misshapen figure before him and shuddered.

"I find that very hard to believe," he said.

"Believe what you like," snarled Hyde . . . and slammed the heavy door in their faces.

Tom Tompkins looked over Enfield's shoulder at the check. Reading was not one of Tom's accomplishments.

"What's it say?" he asked.

"It says "Pay the bearer the sum of ninety pounds'," said Enfield, "and it's signed Dr. Henry Jekyll."

"Who's he?" Tom wanted to know.

"Henry Jekyll is one of the most respected and eminent young professors in London," said Enfield grimly. "He is also engaged to my cousin."

THREE

Enfield was outside the bank before it opened. He firmly expected the check to bounce. When it didn't, he hurried immediately to the home of a friend and adviser of both Dr. Jekyll and himself, John Utterson.

Utterson was a lawyer, a dry, pedantic man whose spare exterior held a warm heart which, although he was at pains to conceal it, frequently got the better of his head.

"I simply can't fathom it, Utterson," said Enfield. "How Jekyll can be duped by this man is beyond me. He is undoubtedly the lowest form of human life it has ever been my misfortune to encounter. What can he and Jekyll possibly have in common?"

"Very little, I should say," replied the lawyer. "But you know Henry. The man is so unworldly as to be almost a saint. Anybody could pull the wool over his eyes. If his father hadn't left him all that money he wouldn't have two halfpennies to rub together, what with his research and the fact that he spends so much time on his charity cases."

"You don't suppose," said Enfield, the words sticking in his throat, "you don't suppose this man could be blackmailing Henry, do you?"

Utterson broke into a bellow of laughter that turned into a coughing fit.

"My dear Richard," he wheezed, "blackmail Henry Jekyll? On what grounds? Why, the man hasn't a vice in the world."

"I know . . . but still . . ."

"You're worried about Mary. That's it, isn't it?"

Enfield nodded.

"In a nutshell," he said. "You know how I feel about her . . . I had always hoped . . . but there—she chose Henry instead and her happiness is all that interests me. But if . . ."

"But if Henry should have some deep, dark secret, that would alter matters?"

"It most certainly would."

"All's fair in love and war—eh, Richard!"

Enfield bridled.

"I find your implications most unfair," he said. "Mary is my cousin, after all. Her welfare is my sole concern."

"Of course it is, of course it is." Utterson was conciliatory. "But aren't you making rather a mountain out of a molehill? This person claims to be Jekyll's best friend. But you haven't heard Henry's side of it. Undoubtedly he has no more than a nodding acquaintance with Mr. . . . . what's his name?"

"Hyde."

The lawyer blanched.

"Hyde?" he said. "Not . . . Edward Hyde?"

"The same. You know him?"

"I know his name," said Utterson. "And you say he is a person of low character?"

"The lowest. He is the scum of the earth, the dregs at the bottom of the bottle, the . . ."

"I think I'm getting the idea."

"Should you need further proof of the type of man he is, come with me now. See the child for yourself. I was just about to go and give the money to the mother."

Utterson reached for his overcoat.

"Lead on," he said.

* * *

On arrival in Soho, Enfield went directly to the address Tompkins had given him the night before.

It was a tall, dingy house in an even dingier alleyway.

The old woman on the ground floor directed them to an attic room four floors above street level. It was bitterly cold. Their breath rose before them like spun sugar as they climbed the rickety stairs.

Enfield knocked on the peeling door.

There was no reply.

He knocked again.

From inside the room came a small whimpering sound like the cry of a kitten stuck in a holly bush.

Enfield pushed the door gently. It swung inwards on creaking hinges.

The child lay on a filthy cot in the clothes she had been wearing the night before. One thin blanket was all that covered her thin body. The folded floursack supporting her was stained with blood from the oozing wound in the back of her head. She had a nasty purplish bruise on her temple and her eyes were swollen and puffy from crying.

The room was even colder than the stairwell. Frost cloaked the skylight and an icy wind whistled under the eaves.

Dolly Coates was nowhere in sight.

Enfield crossed to the bed and knelt beside the little girl. He took one of her small hands between his large ones. The fingers were blue with cold. Enfield chafed them to try to get the circulation going.

"Hello, Daisy," he said gently. "Where's your mother. Has she gone out?"

Daisy looked up at him uncomprehendingly. She was clearly delirious. Her eyes had a bright feverish quality and two blood-red spots stained the pallor of her cheeks.

A sudden convulsion passed over her face and she tried to pull her hand back. Then she began to cry, great racking sobs that shook her entire body.

"Go 'way," she begged. "Go 'way."

Enfield beckoned Utterson over.

"This is Hyde's handiwork," he said. "Justify it if you can . . . and he was caught in the act. Heaven only knows what outrages he might have perpetrated had her mother not arrived when she did."

The older man was visibly moved.

"Dreadful. Dreadful," he muttered hoarsely. "Where is the mother now?"

"Where is your mother, Daisy?" asked Enfield. "Don't be afraid. No one's going to hurt you."

But Daisy had heard that phrase before—the night before—and hearing it brought back the memory and the nightmare.

She began to cry more loudly.

Enfield looked helplessly at Utterson.

"What shall we do?" he said.

Utterson removed his overcoat and wrapped it round the child.

"Well, we can't leave her here, that's for sure," he said. "She won't last the day out."

"What's going on? What you doing to Daisy?"

It was the old lady from downstairs.

"Where's her mother?" said Enfield. "Why has she left the child alone in this condition?"

"She's at the pub, ain't she?" said the woman. "She gave me sixpence to keep an eye on the kid."

"And a wonderful job you're making of it," said Utterson bitterly.

He bent and scooped the howling Daisy into his arms.

"Here," the old woman protested. "You can't do that. Where you taking her? What'm I going to say to Dolly when she comes back and finds the kid's gone?"

"I doubt she'll even notice," said Utterson. "But if she should ask, you can tell her that the gentleman who collected the check has taken her to see Dr. Henry Jekyll."

* * *

What with the soothing motion of the cab and the warmth of Utterson's overcoat, Daisy had fallen asleep by the time they drew up outside Dr. Jekyll's home.

It was a sizeable sandstone house set in a quiet square.

Poole, the butler, opened the door.

He ushered them through the hall, past several charity cases who were huddled round the roaring fire awaiting the doctor's attention, and into the library, where he invited them to make themselves comfortable and assured them that he would inform the master of their arrival.

They didn't have long to wait.

Utterson had just deposited the still sleeping Daisy on a daybed in the corner when Jekyll bounced in full of smiles and handshakes.

Dr. Henry Jekyll was a man it was impossible not to like. He had an honest, open face and an engaging manner. His way of sweeping people along in his enthusiasm made him very difficult to resist.

He was tall, though not quite as tall as Enfield, and handsome in the classical sense. His eyes were blue, his hair was fair, his nose straight, his smile wide and welcoming. His hands were pianist's hands, the fingers long and tapering and ending in perfectly symmetrical, square-cut nails.

"Richard," he said. "John. What a pleasant surprise."

Unhooking his stethoscope and jamming it in the pocket of his white coat, he bounded to the drinks cabinet.

"Let me get you something," he said. "A little brandy, perhaps?"

"Isn't it rather early?" protested Utterson.

"Purely medicinal," chuckled Jekyll. "To keep out the cold."

"Well . . . if you insist."

"Oh, but I do . . . doctor's orders."

He poured two large snifters into balloon glasses and handed them to his friends.

"Not joining us?"

"You know I never drink on duty, Richard. Besides, I still have one or two patients to see."

"We've brought you another," said Utterson.

"Indeed?" Jekyll sounded intrigued.

Utterson indicated the bundle on the daybed.

"A child," he said. "She's had a bad scare. She has a head wound and may well be suffering from pneumonia."

Jekyll's smile slipped the merest fraction, became momentarily less spontaneous, more strained.

"Well, well," he said. "Let's have a look, shall we?"

He moved to the daybed and gently teased the fabric of Utterson's overcoat back from Daisy's bloodstained head.

His reaction was immediate and violent. He dropped the coat as though it were red hot and stepped back hurriedly. He turned, his face drained of blood. He put his hand to his head and swayed unsteadily on his feet.

Enfield moved to support him.

"Are you all right, Henry?" he asked. "You look as though you'd seen a ghost."

Jekyll pushed his friend's hand aside.

"How did this happen?" he croaked.

"She was molested," said Utterson.

"By a friend of yours," said Enfield.

"A man," said Utterson, "known as Edward Hyde."

Jekyll ran his fingers inside his wing collar as though it had suddenly begun to choke him.

"I don't believe it," he said.

"Then you do know this . . . creature?" Enfield was outraged.

"He cannot deny it," said Utterson quietly.

"I do not deny it," admitted Jekyll.

"How could you, Henry?" asked Enfield. "How could you have anything to do with such a . . . a . . . bounder?"

"The situation is too complicated for me to explain," said Jekyll.

"But it needs an explanation nonetheless."

"Perhaps. But just now the important thing is the child. She must have treatment straight away."

Again he lifted the coat from Daisy's face.

The action woke her. She turned her head and smiled sleepily up at him.

"Lo," she said.

Jekyll placed a cool hand on her bruised forehead. She winced and he winced in sympathy.

"Hello, Daisy," he said, and his voice had that resonant, mesmeric quality that all the best doctors possessed. A quality that inspires total confidence in the patient. "Just relax," he said. "My name is Dr. Jekyll and I'm going to make you well."

* * *

Utterson waited in Henry Jekyll's library for another three hours.

He waited until Daisy's wounds had been tended and she had been bathed and fed and tucked up in the spare room by Mrs. Johnson, Jekyll's clucking housekeeper. He waited while Jekyll saw the rest of his charity patients. He waited long after Enfield had given up and headed off for Soho to hand over the ninety pounds reluctantly to the undeserving Dolly Coates.

He waited, in short, until early afternoon, missing his lunch and several important appointments.

But he was determined that he would not leave until he had a few words in private with Dr. Henry Jekyll.

At last the doctor came in, massaging his forehead with fatigue. He looked startled to see Utterson, and not entirely pleased.

"What, still here, John?"

Utterson nodded.

"I wanted a few quiet words with you, Henry," he said. "About the will."

Jekyll sighed. "Ah, yes. The will."

He walked to the drinks cabinet and poured himself a small sherry, offering the bottle to Utterson, who declined. Then he came back to sit facing the lawyer on the opposite side of the fireplace.

"You know I had reservations about the will when I drew it up?" said Utterson.

"I know."

"I explained that it was most irregular that you should leave all your considerable wealth to someone of whom I had never even heard."

23

"You advised me most correctly, John, and I chose to ignore that advice. It is my will, after all . . . and my money."

The lawyer leant forward to place a paternal hand on the younger man's knee.

"You cannot blame me, Henry. I feel responsible for you. I promised your father on his deathbed that I would look out for you."

"And so you always have."

"You are a very rich man, Henry. If—God forbid—you should die young, then the beneficiary of your will would become very rich too. Before I knew the nature of your beneficiary I was worried that the money might fall into the wrong hands. Now that I have heard of his character, I am appalled."

Jekyll stood up.

"Really, John," he said, and his voice was strained, agitated. "You take too much on yourself. I must ask you not to pursue this matter further."

"But you state in your will that should you die or 'disappear', all your wordly goods should go to your 'friend and benefactor', Edward Hyde."

"That is so."

"Your 'friend and benefactor'? You call such a monster your friend and benefactor? To all intents and purposes he is an immoral rogue."

"Enough, John."

"Has he coerced you into drawing up the document against your own free will?"

"No. He has not."

"When you gave him that check last evening, did you know that he wanted it to buy the silence of that unfortunate child's mother?"

Jekyll's face reddened.

"How can you think such a thing?"

"Then what in God's name have you in common with this creature?"

"Nothing," shouted Jekyll. "Everything."

He leant over the startled lawyer, his expression a mixture of anger and elation.

"Listen to me, John," he said. "I will say this only once, and then I forbid you to raise the subject again. I have a great interest in Edward Hyde. His welfare is of supreme importance to me. As my friend I don't expect you to understand this but as my lawyer I expect you to accept it. The will stands."

"And that is your last word?"

"Positively."

The lawyer rose. He looked the young doctor straight in the eye.

"Are you being perfectly honest with me, Henry?"

"As honest as I know how to be."

Utterson sighed.

"Then we shall say no more about it," he said.

Jekyll seemed relieved. He took his friend's hand and pumped it vigorously.

"Thank you, John," he said. "I appreciate it."

He led the lawyer to the door.

"I'm having a little dinner party next week. Just a few close friends. Mary and her father, Enfield, Lanyon . . . I'd be delighted if you could join us."

Utterson smiled.

"It would be my pleasure," he said.

* * *

But it was with a very heavy heart that the lawyer made his way back to his rooms. For he knew that his friend, whom he had never known to tell a lie, had not been truthful with him.

Henry Jekyll must have been fully aware what the ninety pounds was for. Must have known what Hyde had done—and thereby condoned it.

Must have known about the child all along.

How else—when neither he nor Enfield had mentioned it—could he have addressed her by her name and called her "Daisy"?

FOUR

It was well past eight on the evening of the following Thursday that Utterson presented himself at Dr. Jekyll's door.

He could see by the assortment of coats in the cloakroom that the rest of the party were already assembled.

"Am I the last, Poole?" he enquired as the butler relieved him of his top hat.

"You are, sir. Miss Mary and Sir Danvers arrived but a few moments ago."

Utterson handed the butler his overcoat.

"Will . . . Mr. Hyde be dining with us this evening?"

Had the lawyer suggested that they might be joined at the table by a warthog, Poole's reaction could not have been more unfavorable. A fleeting expression of disdain passed across his normally imperturbable features.

"Good heavens no, sir," he said. "Mr. Hyde never uses the main part of the house. He comes and goes by the back door—the one that leads to the laboratory."

"You don't like the man, Poole?"

"It is not for me to like or dislike him, sir. Mr. Hyde is a friend of the master."

"But you don't like him?" persisted Utterson.

"Orders are that we should extend him every courtesy," said Poole, deftly avoiding the question. "Fortunately we do not see the gentleman very often. He has his rooms, I believe" (here he curled his lip in distaste) "somewhere in Soho."

"And what of Miss Daisy?" asked Utterson, changing the subject.

"Much improved, sir. Mrs. Johnson was sorry to see her go. Her mother came to collect her this morning."

He sniffed. Clearly Dolly Coates was another person of whom Poole did not approve.

"John."

Jekyll's voice boomed from the other end of the hall. He strode towards the lawyer and flung his arm around the older man's shoulder.

"Dinner in ten minutes, Poole," he instructed, and ushered the late arrival past his consulting-rooms and the library and into the warmth of the drawing-room.

"You know everyone, I think?" he said. "Look, Mary. Here's John Utterson."

Utterson crossed to where Jekyll's fiancée sat toasting her crimson slippers by the fire.

Mary Carew was a girl of spirit, quite unlike the consumptive types beloved of contemporary poets. The lawyer bent to kiss her hand and she gave him one of her heart-stopping smiles, crinkling up her sea-green eyes in genuine pleasure. Her dark copper hair flashed in the firelight and Utterson thought that, were he twenty years younger, he should be quite as besotted with her as both Jekyll and Enfield obviously were. Even Dr. David Lanyon, a confirmed bachelor, paid her more than normal attention.

Beside her, her father, Sir Danvers Carew, nodded his white leonine head and stuck out a paw in greeting.

"Good to see you, Utterson," he growled.

"And you, sir."

Utterson shook hands briefly with Richard Enfield and paused to exchange a few words with Lanyon, whom he hadn't seen for a while.

Lanyon had been at medical school with Jekyll and the two had remained firm friends ever since. He was a corpulent young man with a high color and a fashionable practice in Harley Street. Lacking Jekyll's brilliance and flair he had, by contrast, a great deal of business acumen and was much sought after in society circles.

"I really must apologize for my late arrival," said Utterson, gratefully accepting the glass of sherry which Jekyll pressed into his hand. "I was detained on a legal matter of some urgency."

Mary laughed.

"You couldn't have timed it better, Mr. Utterson," she said. "Henry has been boring us half to death with a lecture on the nature of good and evil."

"The latest hobbyhorse," grinned Lanyon, "in a long line of hobbyhorses."

"I am surrounded by philistines," complained Jekyll. "Come, John, I need an ally. As a lawyer you deal daily with right and wrong. Tell me. Who is the most evil person with whom you have ever come in contact?"

Utterson deliberated for a moment.

"Probably Atkinson, the ax murderer," he said.

"Ah yes, he was a nasty one," agreed Lanyon.

"Didn't he do away with fourteen women?" asked Mary with a shudder.

"Fifteen," said Utterson. "Dissected them in his butcher's shop and made them into meat pies."

"That must put an end to your theory, Henry," grunted Sir Danvers. "Chap can't have had a single redeeming feature."

"Oh, I don't know," said Utterson. "By all accounts he was extremely fond of his mother."

"You see," crowed Jekyll. "That's my point exactly.

Even the worst of us have some good in us, even the best some bad."

"Maybe that's why he's made a friend of Edward Hyde," said Enfield under his breath to Utterson. "To see if there's any good in him."

"I simply maintain," said Jekyll, who hadn't heard, "that you should be able to dissociate the two elements in man, one from another."

"Physically, you mean?" scoffed Lanyon.

"Why not?"

"Can't be done, old man."

"But suppose it could," Jekyll went on, his eyes alive with enthusiasm. "Think of the advantages for mankind. If you could separate evil and then eliminate it. The possibilities for the good of the world are endless."

"Dinner is served."

Poole's voice cut across the hum of argument.

"Let's hope it's not meat pie," said Mary, and everyone laughed.

And there the conversation ended.

At least for the time being.

But after an excellent meal of oysters and pheasant had been consumed and several bottles of Jekyll's best claret demolished, the discussion resumed in earnest over the coffee and cigars.

Utterson declined to join in, choosing instead to sit back and watch with growing concern as Jekyll put himself, one at a time, in bad favor with everyone in the room.

Sir Danvers, being a man of the old school, was of the opinion that talk of meat pies and murder was hardly suitable matter for the delicate ears of young ladies, and suggested that his daughter might like to retire to the parlor while the gentlemen continued their conversation over the port.

But Mary would have none of it.

"Don't be such an old fuddy-duddy, Father," she teased. "This is the nineteenth century, not the middle ages . . . though I do wish you'd change the subject, Henry," she appealed to Jekyll. "I'm becoming mortally tired of this obsession of yours."

"I thought you of all people would understand," protested Jekyll. "Think of it, my dear. If we could eliminate evil from the human race, at a blow we could obliterate crime, cruelty, violence, vice, war . . ."

Enfield, who was wearing the dress uniform of his regiment, rose to the bait.

"I say, Henry. Surely you acknowledge that war, at least, is a necessary evil."

"Why?"

"Why? Well, because . . . to establish British supremacy, of course."

"And what's so good about British supremacy?"

Now it was Sir Danver's turn to be outraged.

"Really, Henry," he said. "You go too far."

Mary tried to lighten the atmosphere.

"Why, Henry," she said jokingly. "You yourself are living proof that your theory doesn't hold water. How can you say that man is composed of good and evil when you haven't an ounce of wickedness in you?"

Jekyll grabbed her hand across the table, crushing it tightly in his own in a sudden, violent movement. His eyes had taken on a fanatical gleam.

"Oh, but you're wrong, Mary," he said. "Quite wrong. I have my evil side. We all have."

"Henry," protested his fiancée. "You're hurting me."

Jekyll let go of her hand and gave a strained laugh. "You see?"

"This conversation has gone far enough." Sir Danvers struggled to his feet. "Come, my dear," he said to his daughter. "It's time we went home."

Mary massaged her hand.

"Don't be angry, Father," she said. "Henry didn't mean it."

"How do you know I didn't?"

"Oh, Henry, please don't make things worse."

"If we're to be married in three months, my dear, then it's best you know that I *have* my evil side." Jekyll went on regardless. "We all have. Even you."

"This is preposterous," snorted Sir Danvers. "Have a care, Jekyll. If you continue in this vein you may find the wedding plans are off. I may withdraw my consent."

"Father!"

"No, Mary, it's no good. I should be failing in my duty as a parent if I permitted my only daughter to marry a . . . a . . . crank."

"Come now, Uncle," protested Enfield, torn between elation and pity at Mary's distressed expression. "Hang it all, it's only a harebrained theory."

"And Henry has always been known for his harebrained theories," laughed Lanyon. "This one will pass, no doubt . . . like all the others."

"Don't patronize me, Lanyon." Jekyll was suddenly furious. "I am perfectly serious. I not only *believe* that good and evil can be separated in man, I *know* it!"

"Then I suggest you write a paper on the subject to the Royal College, old man," sneered his friend. "Though I shouldn't recommend it. Not unless you want to be laughed out of the profession."

"I shall do more than that," said Jekyll. "I shall

produce a formula that will physically divide the two elements."

"Physically?"

"Exactly."

"I've heard witchdoctors make more sense." Lanyon's voice was icy with scorn.

Jekyll rose to his feet.

"I shall produce proof. I have been experimenting for some time now and all my tests lead me to believe that my theory is correct."

"You need a rest, Henry," said Lanyon. "As your physician I recommend that you take an immediate break from your work. You are clearly not in full possession of your senses."

Jekyll's eyes narrowed and his voice sank to a whisper.

"What has become of you, David?" he said sadly. "What has become of that thirst for knowledge, of that keen, enquiring mind you had when we were at college?"

"I grew up," said Lanyon stiffly.

"You gave up," said Jekyll. "You have joined the ranks of the establishment. There is nothing left for you now but a succession of silly society ladies searching out a cure for their boredom. You have become a quack."

Utterson looked around the table at the distraught and embarrassed faces and back at Jekyll, the defiant host, flushed and unrepentant.

He folded his napkin carefully and rose to his feet with a little cough.

"We have eaten an excellent meal," he said diplomatically, "and drunk perhaps too liberally of Henry's superb wine, and I, for one, am ready for bed. Thank you, Henry, for a most . . . informative evening."

The rest of the party took their cue gratefully, calling for their coats and their carriages.

But Jekyll insisted on having the last word.

He flung it at their retreating backs as they made their way down the garden path to the front gate.

"You shall live to see me proved right, Lanyon," he shouted. "Good and evil *can* be separated."

FIVE

As soon as his guests had departed, Dr. Jekyll instructed Poole that in no circumstances was he to be disturbed. Then he made his way up to his laboratory at the back of the house.

He was in a fine fury.

"Stupid buffoons," he thought. "Mindless morons."

What did they know of good and bad; right and wrong? Pompous, theorizing asses. He'd show them. He, who had confronted evil face to face and become its master. He'd certainly show them.

He fumed his way up to the first-floor landing.

He'd wanted to show them then and there, to hurl their taunts back in their unbelieving faces, to present them with the living, breathing proof of his experiments.

The shame of it.

The humiliation.

That they should suggest he was mad.

He—Henry Jekyll, the man who would rock the whole of the medical establishment back on its self-congratulatory heels.

Soon—very soon.

There were still a few things left to be done, of course. Still a few wrinkles to be ironed out. He had isolated one element. Now all he had to do was pinpoint the other.

He had to admit he was taking a chance, experimenting on himself.

But what else could he do? Whom else could he trust with his secret? No one. Not even Mary.

Tonight had proved that.

Until he had completed his work he could take no one into his confidence.

He could not afford to become a laughing stock.

He must present it to them entire.

The proof.

Without a shadow of a doubt.

He flung the door open and marched into the laboratory.

* * *

"What's to be done?" asked Enfield.

"Nothing," said Lanyon. "He can get himself out of this one. I'll have none of it."

"But Mary's in a dreadful state."

"Better she should find out now that he's unbalanced than after they're married."

Utterson intervened.

"Hardly unbalanced, surely," he said. "A little too much port, perhaps? The drink talking rather than Henry."

"I said unbalanced and I meant unbalanced." Lanyon was unrepentant. "He always had a habit of going off half-cocked. Forever getting into scrapes at college. Can't remember the number of times I bailed him out. And this is the thanks I get. Insulted for my pains."

"Heat of the moment," said Utterson. "All be forgotten in the morning."

"Not by me it won't," said Lanyon grimly. "I've had enough. I'm finished with the man."

"It's this fellow Hyde I blame," cut in Enfield. "Bad influence on Henry, if you ask me."

36

"Hyde?" said Lanyon. "Never heard of him."

"New friend of Henry's. Thoroughly unpleasant character. Into everything from what I hear. Drink. Drugs . . . You don't think Henry could be on drugs, do you?"

"It's possible. His behavior tonight was certainly irrational enough."

The swaying cab jolted to a halt in front of Utterson's apartment.

The lawyer stood up.

"My stop, I think," he said, stepping carefully over his companions' feet and out into the lamplit street. "Don't be too hard on Henry," he added. "We all behave badly sometimes. Wouldn't be human if we didn't."

"Easy for you to say, Utterson," snorted Lanyon. "He didn't call you a quack."

"Or say war was evil," nodded Enfield gloomily.

"He's done for me," said Lanyon.

"Poor Mary," said Enfield.

Utterson sighed. Clearly he was wasting his breath. Henry had alienated them both and neither was going to forgive or forget.

"Goodnight, gentlemen," he said.

"Night, John," said Enfield. "Sleep well."

"Night, Utterson," grunted Lanyon, sinking back onto the red plush seat.

Utterson tapped the rail behind the driver with his cane.

"Drive on," he said.

He watched the cab until it disappeared into the murk. Then, instead of letting himself into his rooms, he turned on his heel and went back the way he had come.

* * *

Jekyll locked the door firmly behind him, took off his smoking-jacket and hung it on a hook by his work bench.

In one corner of the room two piebald rats skittered around their cage, otherwise the laboratory was deathly quiet. An antiseptic smell hung in the air, adding to the impression of sterility created by the gleaming retorts and beakers that dotted the bench and lined the shelves. Several glass-fronted cupboards stood against the walls. One housed rows of jars in which floated pickled portions of human anatomy. Here an ear, there a pair of kidneys and, in one instance, a complete fetus. Acids stood sentinel in another cupboard. Poisons, distinguishable by their skull and crossbones symbol, filled a third.

Jekyll ignored them all.

Rolling up the sleeves of his dress shirt, he made his way to an unprepossessing little chest in the corner.

Taking his fob watch from his waistcoat pocket, he used the small key attached to the end of the gold chain to unlock the third drawer down.

Slowly, with infinite care, he removed the contents of the drawer and placed them on his work-bench.

His hands shook slightly as he dealt out several small square envelopes of paper, each of which held a precisely measured amount of a certain mineral salt. Next came a vial half full of a strong-smelling, blood-red liquid. And finally a well-thumbed book with the inscription "J-H Experiments."

He opened the book at the last entry, which had been written up a week previously. It recorded the quantities of ingredients used in the experiment and one other single word only—Daisy.

Beginning a new page, Jekyll wrote the date, checked

his watch and recorded the hour—it was twenty minutes after midnight—and entered the number of the experiment—thirty-two.

Taking a graduated glass from one of his shelves, he secured it in a clamp and emptied the contents of one of the paper envelopes into it. Then very carefully he measured several drops of the red solution onto the powder.

The concoction began to hiss and bubble, to expand and froth. And as it did so, the color changed from crimson to a deep royal purple and finally, as the bubbles evaporated, to a thin, watery green.

Jekyll unclamped the glass, lifting it towards his eyes, staring into its depth as though, like some gypsy's crystal ball, he might read his future in it.

He savored the moment.

How many times had he stood like this before? In mortal fear the first time, and then, as the experiments had grown in number, in mere trepidation, until eventually that too had passed. Now, looking into the green liquid, he anticipated the revolution he knew it would produce with a kind of guilty longing.

Lowering the glass he moved to the mirror that hung above the empty fireplace. He studied his reflection.

Henry Jekyll. Twenty-eight years old. Bachelor. Doctor of medicine. Savior of the world.

Maybe this time good would triumph.

He raised his glass in salute . . . and swallowed the contents.

The taste was foul.

It burned down his gullet and spewed pain into his guts. He clutched his throat in an attempt to stop the dreadful mixture traveling further, but it was too late.

Convulsions racked his body, causing his eyes to bulge and forcing his lips back over his teeth in a gaping grin of agony. His whole frame was changing, his aspect altering, shrinking, undergoing a transformation before his very eyes.

Coarse dark hair began to curl from the backs of his hands, his eyebrows sprouted and his hairline drooped to meet them. His nose started to spread, his neck to shrink and wither, his shoulders to hunch up towards his ears. His trunk became shorter, his arms longer and his legs bowed outwards until his hands swung, ape-like, almost to his knees. And lastly the fair hair began to darken, the even teeth to gap and narrow into points until—two minutes after he had swallowed the potion—Henry Jekyll was no more.

In his place, grimacing and gibbering at his misshappen reflection, stood that embodiment of all that was evil—Edward Hyde.

He surveyed himself with savage glee.

"Free," he crowed. "Free."

He capered around the laboratory on his bandy legs, the now overlong evening dress trousers flapping around his hairy ankles.

He was free.

Free of the namby-pamby limitations placed on him by Jekyll—that well-meaning idiot who thought to rid the world of evil—who hoped eventually to produce an ego that was wholly good.

Jekyll—who had failed again.

Hyde screeched with laughter.

Poor, deluded Jekyll who thought he could control the wickedness in himself and thereby eradicate it.

But Hyde would show him.

Hyde would not be controlled; would do as he pleased. And he pleased to do many things. Many wonderful, wicked things that Henry Jekyll in his wildest dreams could not begin to imagine.

And Jekyll would not dare to betray him. For he was part of Jekyll, after all. The part that Jekyll had suppressed all these years with his good works and his pious intentions and his self-righteous, self-effacing charity.

How could Jekyll admit that within himself lurked the capacity to perform acts of such unmitigated evil that no civilized human being would even think of them? And not only perform them—enjoy them. For that was the thing. Hyde lived life to the full, tasted its excesses, indulged in its sensual delights and enjoyed himself to an extent that Jekyll had never been able to do.

For Jekyll had a conscience.

And Hyde had none.

Hyde could prepetrate any atrocity without a single spark of remorse, sink to any depths without a hint of self-disgust, live life for the sensation of the moment—and the more revolting the sensation, the more depraved, the better he liked it.

He roared with laughter.

Whatever he did—no one would be able to catch him.

For he had the perfect hiding place.

The indecipherable disguise.

Inside somebody else's skin.

Jekyll's skin.

Giggling delightedly to himself, he took the opera cloak from its peg and, swinging it around his heaving shoulders, let himself out into the night.

*   *   *

41

Poole answered the door in his dressing gown. H[e] carried a candle which he lifted high so that the nake[d] flame might illuminate Utterson's features.

"I'm sorry to disturb you at this hour, Poole," apologized the lawyer, "but has Dr. Jekyll retired yet?"

"He's gone to his laboratory, sir, to work. He le[ft] express instructions that he was not to be disturbed."

"I must ask you to override those instructions, Poole[.] It really is imperative that I speak to him."

"I'm very sorry, sir. The doctor is most particula[r] about not being interrupted in the middle of his re[-] search. I couldn't take it upon myself to call him now."

"Then I shall just have to wait," said Utterson.

"But sir," protested Poole. "It's almost one o'clock i[n] the morning."

"I can't help that. I must see Dr. Jekyll as soon as he['s] available."

Poole appealed to him.

"I really can't call the doctor. It would be more tha[n] my job's worth. On the other hand, if you care to take upon yourself to interrupt him, then I can't stop you."

"I'll take that responsibility," said Utterson, makin[g] to enter the house.

"Not this way, sir," protested Poole. "If you come th[is] way he'll know I let you in."

"Then what do you suggest?"

"The back way, sir."

"I beg your pardon?"

"The laboratory is at the back of the house, sir."

"So?"

"If you go round into the alleyway at the back of th[e] house, you will find a back door. It leads up to th[e] master's laboratory. If you knock and the doctor [is] willing to see you then he will admit you himself. If yo[u] should get no response you could try calling up at the window. Further than that I'm afraid I cannot help you, sir."

"This door, Poole . . ."

"Sir?"

"Is it the one to which Mr. Hyde has a key?"

"The very same."

"Thank you, Poole."

"Don't mention it, sir," said Poole and closed the door firmly in his face.

Utterson made his way round to the back of the house.

It was pitch black.

No street lamp penetrated the awful darkness.

No chink of light from the shuttered windows brightened the gloom.

A wonderful place for a murder, thought Utterson, and he shivered, remembering Atkinson, the mad axeman with his bland, baby face and his vacant eyes.

He stepped on something, something furry and yielding that squealed and wriggled beneath his boot. He lifted his foot hurriedly and the rat scuttled past, nipping at his ankle as it went.

Utterson's heart lurched in his chest.

Quite unnerved now, he wondered whether he might not take Poole's advice. Better perhaps to go home and confront Henry tomorrow?

No.

If he did go home he wouldn't sleep.

He simply must see Henry now. He wanted to ask him, directly, whether this fellow Hyde had turned him onto drugs. Lots of doctors did indulge in opium. To settle their nerves. Pressure of work and all that. If he could get to the root of his friend's strange behavior then he might begin to offer some practical help. A trouble shared was a trouble halved, after all.

Pulling himself together, he felt his way along the back wall of the house until he came to the door of which Poole had spoken.

He was just about to knock when there came the grinding of a key in the lock and the door was flung open and out, almost flattening him against the wall.

The figure that emerged was caught in the sudden glare like an actor in a spotlight. Swathed in an opera cloak so long that it trailed in the mud, it gibbered to itself like an organ-grinder's monkey, chuckling with a kind of diabolical glee.

Utterson crouched back in the shadows. As the figure turned to relock the door, he caught a sudden, tantalizing glimpse of the face.

A wave of pure evil seemed to wash over him. And in that split second, as the hairs rose on the back of his neck, he realized that this could be only one person, the much-discussed and now never-to-be-forgotten Edward Hyde.

Then the door slammed and the light was cut off.

Utterson heard the key turn in the lock, and then the chattering voice retreated into the darkness. He caught the sound of an occasional oath as he stumbled after it, all thoughts of Henry Jekyll forgotten, drawn by the magnetic pull of the malignant presence ahead of him.

Hyde turned into the main road at the end of the alley, hailed a cab and hopped aboard.

As luck would have it, another came bowling by close behind.

Utterson mounted and instructed the driver: "Follow that cab!"

* * *

Twenty minutes later both carriages drew up in a filthy street in the heart of Soho.

Rubbish littered the cobbles and, although it was now well past one, the place was as noisy and lively as though it had been midday.

Women in tattered finery lounged, gossiping, on the corners. Drunks lurched from building to building. Music and light spilled out onto the pavements.

Hyde alighted, paid off the cab and made his way to a private house about three doors down. He rapped on the door with a silver-handled cane and was answered by a woman in a low-cut satin blouse who shrank back at the sight of him. Throwing an arm round her in familiar greeting, Hyde pushed her back inside.

"Where to now, sir?" asked the cabby.

"Wait," said Utterson.

So they waited.

They waited till the moon waned and the hum of the night had shrunk to a murmur. They waited until, one by one, the lords and ladies of the town stumbled home to their various beds. They waited until silence descended on the street and until that silence was broken once again by the twittering of the dawn chorus.

The sun was rising red above the rooftops and driver, horse and passenger had nodded off into uneasy sleep by the time Hyde emerged.

The woman waving him off looked worn and exhausted. Red welts stood out on her arms and she had the first signs of a black eye.

An old, blind beggar lady pulled herself up at the sound of Hyde's approaching footsteps and reached out to touch his arm as he sauntered past.

"Buy a box of matches, kind sir?" she whined.

Hyde swore evilly at her, lifting his cane and bringing

it down with a vicious thwack across her shoulders. She howled at the strength and unexpectedness of the blow.

Hyde shrieked with laughter, grabbed her tray of matches and hurled them into the gutter.

The horse reared at the commotion, shaking Utterson awake. He peered out of the carriage window just in time to see the beggar sink to her knees, scrabbling in the filth for the remains of her livelihood.

Hyde began to kick the matchboxes away from her, splintering them and scattering their pitiful contents to the four winds. Then he trod on the old woman's fingers, accidentally at first and then deliberately, dancing on them like a demented hobgoblin as the unfortunate creature shrieked in pain.

"Hey. Stop that."

Utterson scrambled from the cab, running towards the fallen woman and her attacker.

He grabbed Hyde by the shoulders and swung him around.

The look of unwholesome enjoyment in the man's eyes stopped the lawyer in his tracks, so that, for an instant, he lowered his guard.

It was all the leeway that Hyde needed.

Raising the silver-handled stick in the air, he bought it down on the side of Utterson's head just above the left ear.

Blood spouted and, as his vision clouded, the inscription on the cane's handle swam before the lawyer's eyes.

"To Henry Jekyll," it said, "from his friend, John Utterson, on the occasion of his twenty-first birthday."

* * *

Hyde crept on tiptoe through the back-door.

It was almost six o'clock and he would have to hurry if

he was to get back under Jekyll's skin and into bed before the kitchen maid got up to lay the fires.

He took the stairs three at a time, elated, as he always was, by the night of debauchery culminating in unlooked-for violence.

Tearing off the opera cape and leaving it where it lay, he threw one of the powders into the graduated glass. This time he didn't bother to measure the red liquid. He simply splashed a few drops onto the mineral salts, like a master chef who no longer needs to weigh his ingredients.

He watched the mixture froth and darken. Then he held it up to the mirror and began to chuckle.

He couldn't help it.

It was the thought of Utterson that amused him so. The disbelief on the poor fool's face when the cane had descended. The way that long, mournful face had lengthened even more. The way the mouth had fallen open and the eyes turned in and up as his knees buckled and he fell, pinning that already screeching slut to the ground.

Hyde's body shook with the delicious remembrance of it. He howled hysterically and hugged himself, while tears ran down his face.

He was still screaming with laughter as he swallowed the draught that would turn him back into Henry Jekyll.

SIX

Henry woke that morning with a monumental hang-over.

Sun slanted through a tiny chink in the curtains, falling across his eyes and etching a band of light over the hand that lay beside him on the pillow. He studied the hand through half-closed eyes, examining it with a lazy, dozing scrutiny, noting the dark, curling hairs that sprouted from the back, the obvious strength of the fingers.

And suddenly he was wide awake.

For this was not Henry Jekyll's hand.

He sat bolt upright, holding both hands up in front of his startled face.

These were the hands of Edward Hyde.

Jekyll leapt from his bed and dashed to the wardrobe, flinging the door wide to stare at his reflection in the full-length mirror.

His worst fears were realized.

For the face that stared back at him was not his own.

Something unheard-of had happened.

He had gone to bed as Henry Jekyll—overcome with remorse at the remembrance of Hyde's bestial behavior.

And he had woken . . . as that same Hyde.

Without the aid of the potion, without the use of the formula, he had been transformed overnight from one character to another.

There was a light tap on the door.

"Pardon me, sir, Are you awake?"

It was Poole's voice.

Jekyll swung round in panic.

"Don't come in," he croaked, and the voice was Hyde's voice, mean and thin.

"Are you quite well, sir?" Poole sounded puzzled, as well he might.

Hyde looked about him, searching for a hiding-place. He could scarcely secrete himself in the wardrobe. Instead he rushed to the bedroom door and bolted it.

Poole rattled the knob.

"Dr. Jekyll, sir," he said anxiously. "Are you well?"

"Quite well, thank you," said Hyde, trying in vain to reproduce the tones of Jekyll's voice.

"Mr. Utterson is here, sir," said Poole, "with a policeman. What shall I say to him?"

Hyde's life swam before him.

My God. Utterson. And the police. They had come about last night . . . and then there was Daisy. He cursed himself for not having shown more restraint.

He was caught. Like a rat in a trap. In his own bedroom. With the ingredients for his salvation in the laboratory at the opposite end of the house. He pressed his back against the door, eyes bulging with naked terror, gaping at himself in the wardrobe mirror.

Poole knocked again, more urgently this time.

"Sir?"

"Show them into the library," said Hyde desperately. "Tell them I'll be down directly."

"Yes, sir."

Hyde listened while the sound of Poole's footsteps died away down the hall. Then he cast around for some means of escape. But there was none. The window was too high and there was no back way. No way to the laboratory without going through the house.

There was nothing for it. He would have to brazen it out.

Fear turned to rage—rage to a kind of bravado.

Shooting the bolt back, he opened the door and peered into the corridor.

It was empty.

Stopping only to pick up his watch and chain, he sidled out, almost tripping over the bottom of his pajamas. He bent and rolled the trouser legs up, then continued on his way, slinking from door to door, ears cocked for the sound of any approaching servant.

At last he came to the top of the main staircase leading down into the hall.

From the library he could hear the sound of men's voices raised in conversation.

Gingerly, he made his way down, one step at a time, careful to miss the creaking step fifth from the top.

He had almost reached the bottom when Poole appeared from the direction of the kitchen carrying a tray of coffee.

For one frozen instant the two men faced each other.

Then, with a yell, Hyde took off, catching the astounded butler in the chest with his shoulder, scattering the contents of the tray in all directions. The coffee pot tipped up, splattering the scalding liquid over Hyde's forearms and hands.

He howled in pain and headed off through the house, as though the hounds of hell were after him. Over his shoulder he caught a glimpse of Utterson and a policeman emerging from the library to assist the prostrate butler. Then he was out of the main living quarters, up the stairs and into the safety of his laboratory.

He slammed the door shut, locked it, rushed to the

chest and, with trembling hands, opened the third drawer down.

Grabbing the dirty glass he had used the previous evening, he shook the contents of one of the paper packets into it, sloshed some of the red solution on top and then hopped about, hugging himself with impatience while the mixture began to boil and bubble.

It was still frothing when the policeman arrived outside, closely followed by Utterson and the butler.

They began to bang on the door.

"Go away," screamed Hyde. "Go away, you hell-hounds."

"He's in there," shouted Utterson. "Knock it down."

There came the sound of battering, as though some large shoulder were being heaved against the door. Hyde did a little jig of petrified fury. Would the mixture never change?

"Leave me be, damn you," he yelled. "I have Jekyll here with me. Leave me be or by all that's holy he shall suffer for it."

The banging stopped and, at the same instant, the mixture turned at last to the pale, translucent green.

Hyde hurled it down his throat.

The pangs that racked him were the worst he had ever experienced. He flung himself around the room in agony, banging into the furniture, upsetting glasses, so that, from the outside, it must have sounded as though some knock-down, drag-out fight were occurring in the room.

"Henry!"

It was Utterson.

"Henry! Are you all right?"

Hyde screamed. A last, desperate, dying scream.

"Knock it down, for God's sake, sir." This time it was Poole's voice. "Sounds like they're murdering each other."

Once more came the sound of battering as the three men simultaneously applied their weight to the door. The superstructure could not resist such an onslaught for long. The hinges gave and the door fell into the room with an almighty crash, raising a curtain of dust and rattling the specimens in their jars.

* * *

The laboratory looked as though it had been hit by a hurricane. Shattered glass lay everywhere, upturned retort stands and, in the center of the floor, an opera cloak stained with iodine.

In the midst of the debris, wide-eyed and obviously recovering from some dreadful ordeal, stood Henry Jekyll. He was wearing pajamas and a smoking-jacket.

The back door stood open and the policeman dashed down the stairs in hot pursuit. Of Edward Hyde there was no sign.

Utterson, his head heavily bandaged, rushed into the room.

"Henry," he said, grabbing his friend by the forearms. "Are you all right?"

Jekyll winced.

"Why, sir," said Poole. "Whatever has happened to your hands?"

Jekyll looked down. The backs of his hands were red-raw and covered in blisters.

"It looks like a scald," said Utterson.

"It's nothing," said Jekyll, tucking them into the pockets of his jacket.

"No sign of him, sir," said the policeman, returning

the way he had gone. "It's like he disappeared into thin air."

Jekyll shook his head wearily, like a great bull elephant who has just won a fight for dominion of the herd.

"Oh, he's gone right enough, sergeant," he said. "And he won't be back."

He looked Utterson straight in the eye.

"You have my solemn oath on that."

SEVEN

Jekyll was as good as his word. For the next three months there was neither sight nor sound of Edward Hyde.

Jekyll had had the fright of his life.

On reflection he realized that some unknown quantity was influencing the drug. Quite simply, it was—his own attitude.

Looking back he saw that each time he had taken the mixture he had been in a bad mood. Envy, spite or revenge had been uppermost in his mind.

What had resulted was Hyde.

And now Hyde was developing a mind of his own. Coming forth unbidden. Evil was getting a stranglehold on Jekyll's soul.

He decided that the only way to counteract it was to cease the experiments altogether and concentrate on nurturing the finer side of his nature. If he was diligent enough, then, when he did resume his tests, good should manifest itself rather than evil.

Accordingly, while preparations went ahead for his marriage to Mary Carew, he divided his time between the poor wards and his charity patients. Taking no thought for his health he worked long hours, sometimes far into the night. He read his Bible and tried to harbor no grudges nor have any bad thoughts. He gave up what little he did drink and was frugal in his diet, punishing the flesh to purify the spirit.

In other words, he was a model of propriety.

Mary was delighted.

Even her father stopped complaining about Jekyll's character and grudgingly admitted that he might have been too hasty in his judgement.

All seemed set for a happy future.

Until, on the eve of his wedding, beset no doubt by the nerves experienced by every expectant bridegroom, wishing perhaps for "one last fling" before he bound himself in the fetters of matrimony, Jekyll yielded to temptation and mixed the potion.

Evil, denied for so long, came out roaring like a beast unleashed. All Jekyll's good intentions were overthrown in that instant of rebirth, swamped by Hyde's greed for sensation—any sensation—no matter how repulsive.

It was an early summer's night, the sky darkening from eggshell blue to reddish-purple, the air heady as wine. Hyde drank it in like nectar, savoring the magic of the evening as, in dress clothes and opera cloak, he strutted his way towards Soho, planning his wickedness as he went.

And, as luck would have it, rounding a corner close by his rooms in Soho, whom should he meet but his future father-in-law, Sir Danvers Carew.

The devil in him could not resist the humor of the situation.

He doffed his top hat to the old gentleman and made him a deep, courtly bow.

"Sir Danvers," he said. "How good to see you."

Carew stopped in his tracks, staring at the disreputable figure before him with ill-concealed disdain.

"You have the advantage of me, sir," he grunted. "I don't believe I have had the pleasure."

"Doubtless you have forgotten," sniggered Hyde.

"I assure you, sir, I never forget a face," said Sir

Danvers, his tone indicating that he would certainly not forget such a face as leered at him now.

"When we last met," said Hyde, with a wink, "you were in the company of your charming daughter. Now there's a wench I could honor with my intentions and no mistake."

Sir Danvers took immediate and apopleptic offense.

"How dare you insult my daughter, you scoundrel?" he snorted. "Why if I were ten years younger I'd thrash you within an inch of your miserable life."

He raised his cane.

Hyde snatched it from him and snapped it across his knee. He glanced around. Except for themselves the street was empty.

Normally he would have let the whole thing go with an oath and a threat. But tonight he was eager for confrontation. He decided to do what, as Henry Jekyll, he had often longed to do, but never dared. He decided to teach the high and mighty Sir Danvers a lesson in manners.

Turning the point of his silver-topped cane towards the old man, he prodded him in the chest, driving him back against the wall.

"I call that most uncivil," he snarled. "Raising your cane to someone who meant you no harm."

He tapped the old man on both cheeks with his kid gloves, then chucked him under the chin like a baby, teasing him, savoring his discomfort.

"Leave me be, sir," stuttered Sir Danvers. "Or I shall be forced to call the law."

"I am the law here!" Hyde's voice was menacing. "The judge, the jury . . . and the executioner."

He tapped Sir Danvers sharply on the head, observing

with satisfaction that the discomfort in the old man's eyes had changed to something else—fear, perhaps?

One of Hyde's particular pleasures was to inflict pain, preferably on those smaller and weaker than himself. He felt the urge rising in him to put the fear of God into this old fool. All his life Sir Danvers had been an authoritarian, some would say a bully, imposing his will on others. On Mary. On that soft-centered jelly, Jekyll.

Hyde decided that it was time Sir Danvers had a taste of his own medicine.

He raised his cane threateningly.

The old man looked up, raising an arm to ward off the expected blow. His eyes lit on the silver handle—on its inscription.

Once more his outrage got the better of his good sense. He grabbed at the cane, attempting to wrest it from Hyde's grasp.

"That is Henry Jekyll's cane," he puffed. "How did you come by it . . . you thief?"

"He gave it to me." Hyde grinned evilly. "We share everything."

"Liar," shouted Sir Danvers. "Jekyll would never associate . . ."

"Ah, but he would," interrupted Hyde, leaning closer to his victim, using his superior strength to pin him against the building. "Henry Jekyll and I are the closest of friends. Two peas in a pod. He is closer to me than he is even to the lovely Mary. Why, he has even invited me on his honeymoon." He licked his lips lasciviously. "Who knows that he might not share her with me too?"

"Devil," roared Sir Danvers. "You shall never sully my daughter's company with your foul presence. The wedding is off."

Suddenly Hyde was tired of the game; hated the old man in front of him; hated everything he stood for; hated his power to wreck the lives of Henry and Mary.

He raised his stick and this time he brought it down on Sir Danvers's head, sending his top hat sailing into the gutter.

"The wedding is on, you selfish old fool," he panted, lifting the stick and bringing it down, again and again. "With or without your consent."

Sir Danvers fell to his knees, covering his unprotected head with his arms, trying to deflect the blows.

"No," he pleaded. "No . . ."

"Yes," howled Hyde. "Yes. Yes. Yes . . ."

At first he had just wanted to knock the old man about a bit, give him a fright . . . but as the cane rose and fell he realized that he would never be satisfied until he had laid this thorn in his flesh to rest once and for all.

Time he died anyway. Interfering old swine. Ruining people's lives. Ending their enjoyment. Hypocrite. Superannuated old goat. Putrid, prating parasite.

Hyde took the stick in both hands and, bringing it down with all his considerable strength, split Sir Danvers's skull in two.

The certainty that the old man was dead did nothing to arrest him. Rather it inspired him to new frenzies. Hyde beat and hacked and chopped like a madman.

Over and over the stick thwacked down until it snapped in half in his hand.

Finally, bloodlust spent, he stood pouring with sweat over the unrecognizable mound of flesh that had once been a man.

* * *

From start to finish the encounter had taken no more than ten minutes. Hyde's eyes fell to his hands, his shoes, his clothing. They were saturated with blood. If someone should find him here, in this state, his freedom would be short-lived.

He wheeled around, ready for flight, but there was no one in sight. The street was as vacant and peaceful as before.

Dragging the body into an adjacent doorway, Hyde concealed it under a pile of rubbish.

He scanned the street again.

Still no one.

Luck was with him.

The luck of the devil.

He scurried to the corner, peered around. The next street too was empty.

If he could just get to the other end and round the corner without being spotted he would be at his rooms. Home free. He could dispose of the blood-stained clothing. No one would ever know.

No one had seen him kill Sir Danvers. No one had seen Hyde for months. No one would connect him with the murder.

The perfect crime.

If he could get to his rooms.

A couple entered the street, holding hands, heads together, giggling.

Hyde shrank back against the wall, holding his breath until they passed, oblivious of everything except themselves, lost in their own private world.

He looked.

The street was empty again.

It was now or never.

Fear leant wings to his heels.

He hurtled down the street and round the corner.

Luck was still with him.

It was that time of night when honest folk were already in bed and dishonest folk were still preparing for an evening of evil pursuits. Not a soul was abroad. No one shouted after him as he skittered to the door of his rooms. Nobody hailed him as he scrabbled in his trouser pockets for the key.

The key that wasn't there.

He hammered at the door, his heart pounding painfully in his chest.

If that slut was out at the pub he'd strangle her.

He hammered again.

Where was she, dammit? Didn't she realize this was a matter of life and death?

From inside came the sound of dragging feet.

"Let me in, you good-for-nothing," he raged through the letterbox.

"All right, all right." The voice was fuddled with sleep . . . or drink . . . or both. "Hold your horses."

The lock slid back.

Hyde hurled himself inside, knocking the unfortunate woman back on her heels. He slammed the door and slid the bolt home.

Inside, the house was tastefully furnished, warm and welcoming, with a coal fire leaping in the grate.

Only the woman looked out of place. Even the expensive dress she wore could not camouflage the coarseness of her features, the commonness of her manner. Her face was heavily painted, her thick dark hair struggling to escape from the pins that tried in vain to secure it.

She stared at Hyde in terror, at his dishevelled dress, the blood smearing his face, the hellish excitement in his eyes.

She began to whimper, like a child who knows it is in for a beating.

Hyde did not disappoint her.

He slapped her across the face, a hard, vicious blow that left the imprint of his bloodied hand across her painted cheek.

"Shut up," he snarled.

He was elated with a sense of his own cleverness.

He had got away with it.

He slapped Nancy again for good measure.

She began to cry, biting her lip to hold back the noise but unable to control the tears that welled in her eyes and ran down her face, leaving little rivulets in her rouge.

Her pathetic face acted like a red rag on Hyde.

Grabbing her bony shoulders, crushing them between his strong hands, he pulled her petrified face to his own.

"Ahhhhh, Nancy," he hissed. "My beautiful Nancy. I killed a man tonight. Murdered him with my own bare hands. This blood that you feel against your skin is his. I made it flow. I beat it from his body. And no one knows. No one except you and me. It will be our little secret."

He leant forward to kiss her bloodstained cheek. She shrank back from him but he wouldn't let her go, pulling her closer until her frightened eyes were not an inch from his own.

"And here's another little secret," he said slyly. "If you should ever tell . . . if you should betray my confidence . . . then you know what will happen, don't you?" He smiled but his eyes stayed hard as flint. "I shall kill you, too, Nancy. Remember that if you should ever be tempted to tell. You will remember, won't you, dear?"

The woman nodded dumbly.

"Good girl," said Hyde.

He thrust her from him. She staggered back against the dresser, rattling the bone china cups.

"Now heat me some water," he instructed. "And bring me a change of clothes and a bottle of wine—no, two bottles. I feel like celebrating."

Hyde bathed and changed and got roaring drunk. By the time he left at three in the morning he had regaled Nancy with every revolting detail of the murder of Sir Danvers Carew and his subsequent escape. He reeled off home, congratulating himself on his cunning.

He was so delighted with his night's work that he even toasted the unfortunate Sir Danvers in the transforming potion.

* * *

But for every high there is a corresponding low. And it was to this low that Dr. Henry Jekyll sank when he came to himself in his laboratory.

The depths of his horror and remorse were such that he was torn by physical pain, as though every blow dealt out to Sir Danvers was being revisited upon the striker a hundredfold.

As his memory regurgitated some of the more repulsive parts of the crime, his stomach churned. He staggered to the sink and was violently sick, spewing out the wine to stain the white enamel like the victim's blood. He heaved until there was nothing left and only dry retching tore his throat.

But although the vomiting relieved the pain in his stomach, it did nothing to ease the tearing sickness that he felt in his heart.

He crumpled to the floor and, burying his head in his arms, began to cry like a lost child.

He cried to God to strike him dead and thus relieve him of the agony of guilt and misery that he felt.

When no answering thunderbolt met his desperate pleas, he took the key to the back door and broke it in two, sealing forever Hyde's exit to the outside world.

EIGHT

The body was discovered some hours later by a tramp scrounging for leftovers.

But such was the horrifying condition of the corpse that it was several hours more before it was positively identified.

The police, called to the scene, could deduce only that the victim had been a man of a certain height and a certain age and that, from the quality of the cloth in what was left of his well-cut suit, he seemed to have been a gentleman.

Then one enterprising young constable, with a slightly stronger constitution than the others, found, while searching the remains, a letter addressed to the lawyer, John Utterson.

Utterson was roused from his bed to a scene which made him profoundly grateful that he had not waited to eat breakfast.

In his years as a lawyer he had seen many appalling sights, but none as revolting as the state of the poor wretch on the pavement.

Even the police, indifferent in the face of the most repulsive of crimes, were strangely silent, avoiding each other's eyes in the presence of such wickedness, and several, who had long ago considered their insides to have the consistency of cast iron, were looking distinctly green around the gills.

Utterson broke the seal on the envelope and, from the signature on the will within, which had just been changed in Dr. Henry Jekyll's favor, was devastated to discover that the body was none other than that of Sir Danvers Carew.

He was also able to identify the broken silverheaded stick found in the gutter hard by the body's place of concealment.

"Motive and incriminating evidence." The police inspector—one James Watson—could not have been more content. "I think it's time we paid a visit to Dr. Henry Jekyll."

Utterson leapt to his friend's defense.

"No, no, inspector," he said. "I fear you've got hold of the wrong end of the stick."

The inspector raised an eyebrow and Utterson, apologizing for his tactless choice of expression, hurried on.

"This can have nothing to do with Jekyll. This is the work of some lunatic. Only a total degenerate could perpetrate such a villainous act. And Henry Jekyll is the finest of men."

"Then why is his cane here, sir, at the scene of the crime, covered in the victim's blood?"

"It's his cane, I cannot deny that, but to my certain knowledge Jekyll hasn't had it in his possession for months."

"Indeed? And in whose possession has it been?"

"A blackguard called Hyde. A worse rogue you could never hope to meet. It's my opinion that he stole it."

"And you're entitled to your opinion, I'm sure, sir. But we shall still have to see Dr. Jekyll and hear his side of it."

"But it couldn't have been Henry. Why, he's due to be married today."

"Does that have some relevance, sir?"

"I fear so." Utterson turned cold at the thought. "He

was to be married to the daughter of that . . . that unfortunate object on the pavement."

And so it was that while Utterson accompanied Inspector Watson and his sergeant to Henry Jekyll's house, the young constable who had found the letter in the first place was given the unenviable task of going to the home of Mary Carew to tell her that her father was dead and her fiancé suspected of brutally murdering him.

NINE

Henry woke with his heart in his mouth and that feeling of foreboding which lingers in the wake of a particularly horrific nightmare. But it was not until he heard the raucous voice of the news vendor crying "Murder" in the square outside that the full horror of the previous evening's events came flooding back.

It was his wedding day.

Sir Danvers Carew was dead, and by now Mary would know.

How could he face her? What could he say? He would have to give her her freedom. Now, when she needed him most, how could he comfort her grief knowing that a part of him, the foulest part, was responsible for her father's death?

On him lay the blame.

He had let the monster loose.

His agony was interrupted by a commotion at the front of the house, loud hammering and upraised voices.

Henry clambered out of bed, crossed to the bedroom door, eased it open a hair's breadth and applied his ear to the opening.

Downstairs he could hear Poole padding across the hall, then the creak of the front door opening, followed by an exchange of conversation. Utterson's clear pedantic accents were distinguishable from some others which he failed to recognize.

He tiptoed along the landing and looked over the

banisters, seeing but not being seen, hearing without being heard.

It was the police.

They stood in the lower hall alongside Poole and Utterson: a man in a brown derby, clearly in charge, and several uniformed constables.

"The doctor is still in bed, sir," Poole was saying.

"Then kindly rouse him," instructed the plain-clothes man, "and inform him that Chief Inspector Watson of Scotland Yard would like a few words."

Poole, supremely unimpressed by Watson's credentials, looked to Utterson for guidance.

"Mr. Utterson, sir? You haven't forgotten that the doctor and Miss Carew are to be married this afternoon?"

Utterson shook his head glumly.

"I'm afraid the wedding will have to be postponed, Poole."

"Postponed? I don't think I quite follow you, sir."

"Sir Danvers Carew was murdered last night."

"Beaten to death," said Watson with relish, "with Dr. Jekyll's walkingstick."

Henry waited to hear no more.

He fled back into his room and turned the key in the lock.

His stick. My God, they had come for *him*. They had found his stick and put two and two together to make five. They thought he, Jekyll, had done it.

This was something he hadn't bargained for. Jekyll, not Hyde, accused of murder.

Fear dried his mouth.

It wasn't fair.

He hadn't done it.

Why, he wouldn't hurt a fly.

They couldn't accuse him. An innocent man.

He was innocent. Innocent. Hyde was the one who had done it. Hyde was the culprit!

As before, when he had been trapped in this room with the police below, Henry's eyes lit on his reflection in the wardrobe mirror. This time it was Jekyll who glared back, his features uncharacteristically twisted by fear. Jekyll, trapped like an animal awaiting the huntsman's kill.

Or was it?

Something sly and knowing peeped out at him from behind Jekyll's eyes.

"Innocent?" the look said. "Are you quite sure?"

The eyes bored into him. "Hypocrite!" they mocked. "You *are* Hyde. You are guilty. Guilty of murder in the first degree. You—and I—we are all to blame."

Henry began to shake.

"No," he croaked. "It isn't true."

Great shuddering convulsions began to rack his body. And still the all-seeing, all-knowing eyes pierced through him, accusing. You did it. You. Jekyll and Hyde.

With a superhuman effort of will Henry tore his gaze away from the eyes behind the eyes. He looked down at his hands. Black hairs were beginning to sprout from the backs.

He was changing.

"Dear God," he gasped.

"Henry." The voice coming from Jekyll's mouth was Hyde's. "It is me. I am here. Let me through."

Jekyll sank to his hands and knees, panting like a dog, shaken by rigors as the fierce battle for identity raged through his tortured body.

"Leave me be," he groaned—and this time the voice

69

was his own. "I won't become Hyde. I am Henry Jekyll. I am me."

"It is Henry Jekyll they seek," rasped Hyde. "Jekyll's cane they found. Jekyll they believe committed the murder. If, when they open the door, they discover Edward Hyde, then all will be well. Self-preservation, my dear Henry, that is the name of the game. So come along . . ." the voice was enticing now, "let me out."

"And leave my body and soul to your tender mercies? I'd die first."

"Dr. Jekyll."

Poole's voice was followed by a light tap on the door. Henry froze.

The eyes behind the eyes retreated. The shuddering stopped. The hairs retracted into their follicles.

"Dr. Jekyll, sir." Poole rapped again.

Henry crouched lower, his stomach scraping the carpet, trying not to breathe.

"Dr. Jekyll, are you awake, sir?"

Poole knocked a third time. He tried the door. The handle rattled. The key did a little jig in the keyhole. "Dr. Jekyll. Are you there?"

Henry bit his lip, containing Hyde's gibbering, preventing him from calling out and giving the game away. He bit until the blood came and until, after several more minutes of knocking and importuning, the rattling ceased and Poole retreated.

Henry let out his breath in a huge whoosh of relief, wiped the blood from his lip and raised his head.

The eyes leapt out at him from the other side of the mirror. Hyde's voice forced its way from between his clenched teeth.

"We have some unfinished business, Henry," it said. The convulsions began again, slowly at first, then

70

building in intensity. Henry fought to control them. Once more the hairs began to curl from the backs of his hands. His hairline slid towards his beetling eyebrows and his teeth sharpened into points.

"No," he protested. "Let me alone."

But Hyde only laughed. And the laughter began to envelope Henry, to swallow and devour him until he was being sucked into a vortex, dragged down to the depths of a bottomless well.

And from the slime of that hellish pit, he looked up and saw . . . Mary.

Her photograph watched him from the dresser. Her dear, sweet face framed in that cloud of Titian hair. Her green eyes smiled out at him, profferring solace, offering sanctuary.

What was left of him reached out to her, pushing Hyde aside to grasp whatever absolution she had to offer.

And Hyde, taken unawares by the depths of Henry's devotion, growled and pulled back to lick the wounds of his damaged ego and gather his forces for a further assault.

In that brief moment of respite, Henry scuttled on hands and knees towards salvation, snatched up the portrait of his fiancée and held it tight against his chest.

Great waves of emotion washed over him and he thanked whatever gods there were for Mary with her strong will and her steadying influence and her innate good sense. Mary, who loved him and whom he loved in return.

And Hyde, unable to withstand such a flashflood of gratitude, was swept away on that tide of feeling into the back reaches of Henry's consciousness.

The convulsions settled, the teeth straightened, the hair curled back under the skin.

Henry flopped back against the dresser, still clutching Mary's likeness. Sweat slicked his forehead, his heart hammered and his knees felt as weak as though he had just climbed Mount Everest.

He had come through a momentous battle. A battle for control of his own soul.

He was exhausted.

But he was alive.

And he was still Henry Jekyll.

He closed his eyes in relief, then snapped them open again as a series of sharp knocks punctuated the calm after the storm.

Absorbed in his crisis, Henry had not heard the police approach. Had he been making a noise? Had they heard him? They were here. Now. Only the bedroom door separated him from his fate.

Panic gripped him once more.

He couldn't face them at this moment. He needed time to think, to prepare his defense—if he had one.

He staggered to his feet.

"Open up in the name of the law."

It was Watson's voice.

"Henry." Now Utterson's. "Henry. It's John Utterson. Open the door, there's a good fellow."

Had they heard him, then? Or had the conflict been a silent one, a play enacted in the confines of his own head? Henry didn't know. He crossed to the window and looked out. The two-story drop looked fearsome. But not as fearsome, he thought grimly, as the drop from the gallows.

Hurriedly, he threw off his pajamas and began to climb into his day clothes.

Outside, voices were raised in debate.

"You're sure he's in there?" The police inspector.

"Not sure at all, sir." Poole. "The master was working in his laboratory until late last evening. I did not see him retire."

"But the door is locked?" This accompanied by more rattling of the knob.

"As you see, sir."

"From the inside?" Utterson, asking a lawyer's question.

There was a brief silence while someone, presumably Chief Inspector Watson, applied his eye to the door.

"Looks like," he said. "The key's still in the keyhole."

"Then why doesn't he answer?" Utterson sounded worried.

"My guess is he doesn't want to."

"Why not? You cannot convince me that Jekyll has anything to do with this matter. Hyde is your man. He's the one who had the stick last."

"What's his motive?"

"He doesn't need a motive. The fellow is capable of anything. I know from sad experience."

Henry pricked up his ears.

Good old John, standing by him in the face of all this. A lump rose in his throat. He didn't deserve such loyalty. Perhaps he should give himself up after all?

No. It was too risky.

He needed time to compose himself.

And if they did begin to suspect Hyde, then he would need to get to Soho and make sure that Nancy had destroyed the bloodstained shirt.

That was it.

He would go to Soho.

No one knew him there.

At least, no one knew Henry Jekyll.

Flicking a speck of dust from his tweed jacket, he picked up his Gladstone bag, clicked it open and took out a sheaf of blank prescription forms.

He wrote a brief message on the top sheet, folding it in half and placing it, in full view, on his dresser by Mary's portrait.

Outside, the debate raged on, interspersed by intermittent hammering and rattling of the doorknob.

"Henry," shouted Utterson, quite out of patience. "For God's sake open this door."

"Perhaps he can't," said Watson ominously.

"I don't follow you . . ."

"Well . . . if he *did* do it . . ." Watson left the sentence hanging by the neck.

"Good lord." Utterson was appalled. "You're not suggesting . . ."

"Stranger things have happened . . . Remorse after the event . . ."

"Do you have a spare key, Poole?" Utterson's voice had take on more than a hint of urgency.

"In the pantry, sir."

"Then get it, man . . . and hurry . . . the doctor may have taken his own life . . ."

The sound of Poole's feet moving faster than they had done in years was followed by a frantic scrabbling as somebody, or perhaps several people at once, attempted to dislodge the heavy key from its niche.

It was time to go.

Methodically, Henry secured the clasp on his doctor's bag.

Coolly, he crossed to the window.

He was calm now, his previous panic spent. He was in control. He knew what he had to do.

He raised the window sash and swung one leg over the sill.

He had never been very good with heights. He mustn't look down.

He swung his other leg over and edged himself carefully along the overhang, dragging the bag behind him.

Luckily his bedroom window was at the side of the house. The police van would be waiting around the corner, outside the entrance, and any curious onlookers would be gathered there.

Henry scrutinized the house next door. No hand disturbed the lace curtains, no face peered inquisitively from behind the shutters.

He aimed the Gladstone bag out and down. It landed with a soft thud on the grass bordering the flowerbed.

Then, taking his courage—and the drainpipe—in both hands, he swung himself off the ledge and slid down into the garden.

* * *

It was Utterson who found the note.

It said merely that Jekyll had been called away on an urgent case at five A.M. that morning and didn't know when he would return. It asked that Poole get word to Miss Carew that the wedding might be forced to have be delayed.

Chief Inspector Watson was not convinced.

The open window, the imprint of the boots in the soft earth beneath the drainpipe and the indisputable fact that the door had been locked from the inside did little to reassure him of Jekyll's innocence.

Despite strong protests from Utterson, he issued an immediate directive to the entire Metropolitan Police

Force ordering that Dr. Henry Jekyll be arrested on sight.

Then, instructing the butler and the lawyer to remain where they were in case of the doctor's return, he set off hastily for Soho and the rooms of Mr. Edward Hyde.

TEN

When Henry reached Soho he did not go directly to his destination. Instead he stepped into an adjacent coffee house and took a table by the window which afforded him a direct view of Hyde's front door. He ordered a pot of coffee, picked up a copy of *The Times* and settled down to pretend to read.

He did not have long to wait.

It was Nancy's habit to visit the King's Arms around eleven o'clock each morning to take a little something to "steady her nerves." Sure enough, five minutes after his arrival she staggered forth, sporting an impressive black eye, and made her way unsteadily into the pub.

Henry watched her progress with a mixture of distaste and pity. Distaste, because she was as far removed from his beloved Mary as chalk from cheese and yet he knew her much better than he did his fiancée. Pity, because he knew how she had come by the black eye.

He allowed another five minutes to give her time to settle down over the first gin of the day, then he paid his bill and let himself into Hyde's house with the key which this time he had been careful to bring with him.

The rooms were untidy, musty with the smell of sweat and stale cigar smoke. The bottles and glasses of the previous evening still lay scattered about the parlor. Henry made his way to the bedroom. At the foot of the rumpled bed lay the evidence that could hang him. Hyde's shirt, stained with blood.

Anger stirred in Henry's breast.

Despite Hyde's express instructions Nancy had apparently gone to bed without first disposing of the evidence of his crime.

Was she lazy, or stupid, or both?

He looked in the closet. There was no sign of the dress suit. That, at least, she had destroyed.

Then why not the shirt?

Was she being devious? Was she retaining the evidence in the hope of some future blackmail?

Henry felt the familiar itching sensation on the backs of his hands. He hoped not. For her sake he sincerely hoped not.

He knelt by the grate and, scraping last night's ashes aside, began to build a hasty fire. Paper. Wood. Coal. He thrust the shirt into the heart of the pyramid and had just struck the match that would set it alight when he heard the key turning in the front door and Nancy's hoarse tones inviting someone in.

The flame from the match seared his fingers.

He dropped it hurriedly in the hearth and, stumbling to his feet, lurched to the bedroom door to listen.

The police had arrived.

Either they had tracked him here or Hyde was already suspect. In any case, if they found him, he was in dire trouble. He looked around wildly for somewhere to hide.

There was nowhere—only the closet and that was too small.

Grabbing the soiled shirt from the grate, he did the only thing left to him. He slid under the bed.

Moments later the door swung open and Nancy's blue-shod feet appeared, accompanied by a pair of highly polished brown boots and several pairs of black.

Henry counted them. One, two, three, four. Four

policemen. Or three and a sergeant. Clearly Chief Inspector Watson was taking no chances.

"He done it." Nancy's voice was slightly slurred by gin. "I know he done it."

Her feet came towards the bed.

"Look, here's the . . ."

The feet stopped.

"What is it? What's wrong?" Henry recognized the tones of Chief Inspector Watson.

"The shirt," Nancy said. "The shirt he was wearing. The one covered in blood. It was here. He told me to burn it, but I never."

"Why?" the chief inspector wanted to know.

"Because I want him caught, don't I? Because I hate his guts."

"Am I," enquired the chief inspector, "addressing Mrs. Hyde, by any chance?"

Nancy's raucous laugh filled the room, setting Henry's teeth on edge.

"Mrs. Hyde? That's a good 'un. Who'd marry him?"

Under the bed Henry felt a dreadful anger growing in him. Ungrateful wretch. After all Hyde had done for her. This house. The clothes. The jewels. The money to indulge her taste in gin. His attempts to educate her in the finer things in life. All wasted.

"He's a monster," she was saying. "A brute. Look at this shiner. And that ain't the first. I bin black and blue with the beatings. He ain't normal. He likes to hurt people."

"But could he commit murder?"

"Could and did. He told me—every detail. Fair made me want to puke."

"And where is he now?"

"Your guess is as good as mine. He comes and he goes.

79

He hadn't been round for a couple of months before last night. Thought I was done with him at last. No such luck."

"Would you give a statement under oath?"

"I daren't." Nancy sounded suddenly afraid.

"Why not?"

"Because of the shirt. It was here and now it ain't. What if he's been back for it? What if he's here—in the house—now? What if he heard me? He'll do for me for sure. Oh, inspector," she wailed. "You gotta help me. The man's a devil. You don't know what he's like when he's roused. I don't want to say nothing."

She began to cry, loud, harrowing sobs, ugly and abandoned.

The sound grated on Henry's nerves. He found himself wanting to leap from his hiding place and throttle the life out of the stupid hussy.

He looked down.

Hairs were crawling like centipedes from the backs of his hands.

He closed his eyes and tried to beat back the hate that threatened to engulf him. How could he expect Nancy to be loyal to Hyde? Everything she said was true. He was a monster. He had made her life a living hell.

Nancy continued to cry.

The chief inspector tried, without success, to calm her.

"Come now, my dear," he said. "There's no need to worry. Just tell us what you know and we'll have the villain behind bars in no time."

"You gotta catch him first."

"We'll catch him, never fear."

"But what if he's in the house?"

"If he was in the house we'd have heard him by now."

Under the bed Henry permitted himself a small, cynical smile.

"What about the shirt?" said Nancy.

"The shirt will turn up, you'll see. Maybe you left it in the parlor. Let's go through and see, shall we?"

The brown boots accompanied the blue slippers to the door.

"What about my protection?"

"You'll get it as of now. Arnold—cover the front door. Potter—you take the back gate. Sergeant, bring your notebook. Miss Walker has some things to tell us."

Henry stayed stock still until the fourth pair of black boots had exited, closing the door behind them, then he crawled from his hiding place and dusted himself down.

He was in a fine fix. Trapped in a house full of police, both exits guarded, and in possession of a bloodstained shirt that could be the death of him.

He tiptoed to the window, peeping through the half-drawn blinds.

The yard was little more than a rubbish dump. Boxes and buckets, an old bathtub filled with empty gin bottles, a rusting baby carriage that had seen happier days.

The top of Officer Potter's helmet appeared suddenly beyond the back gate and began to move backwards and forwards like a duck in a shooting gallery.

Henry shrank back out of sight.

A low wall separated the yard from a similar one next door. If he was bold, he could slip out of the window and over the wall and exit from the adjoining building. No one was looking for him. It was Edward Hyde they were after now.

In the hall he could hear the inspector taking his leave of Nancy.

It was now or never.

He turned back into the room, opened the doctor's bag and began to stuff the soiled shirt inside.

It was at that precise moment that the door swung open and Nancy entered the room.

She stopped dead at the sight of him, her mouth dropping open.

"Who the 'ell . . ." she began.

But she got no further.

Henry dropped the bag, scattering the contents over the bed.

Two bounds took him to her side. He grabbed her roughly by the waist, swung her round and clamped his hand over her mouth.

She struggled but her struggling was futile for Henry could feel great strength welling up in him. And with it came a great fury. And then the familiar feelings that heralded his change began to crowd in on top of him. The shaking and the sweating and the cramp. But this time he was powerless to stop them—did not *want* to stop them as his righteous indignation turned to uncontrollable rage.

"You told them, Nancy," he hissed and the woman's body tensed under his hands at the sound of that almost familiar voice.

She began to quiver, her heart to pump wildly. Henry could feel it pounding through her back as he held her close against his chest.

Suddenly, through his fury, he felt a kind of affection for this sad, silly creature who had such a short time to live. He nuzzled his nose into the slope of her neck, then raised his head slightly to kiss her earlobe.

Over her shoulder he glimpsed the filthy shirt crumpled on the floor. He twisted her head so that she could see it too.

"I warned you what I would do if you told," he whispered.

From a fold in the shirt something glinted, winked at him, beckoned.

Keeping one hand over Nancy's mouth, he loosed his hold on her waist momentarily as he bent to pick up the scalpel.

Nancy bit him, bit down hard until she almost reached bone. Then, as he cursed and drew his hand away, she whirled around to face him.

Her eyes, when she saw him, darkened with recognition and belief in the unbelievable.

For this was not the man she had found in her bedroom, the man with the blue eyes and the tired, kindly face. This was not the man who had grabbed her and covered her mouth with his hand. This was—though it couldn't be—Hyde. Her nemesis and her death.

She opened her mouth to scream.

And Hyde raised the scalpel and, in one clean cut, slit her throat from ear to ear.

The scream was stillborn, drowned in the gush of lifeblood that pumped from her jugular vein, splashing the walls with a fountain of crimson droplets as she fell, in a circular motion, onto the Persian rug.

Hyde watched with a grim smile as her fingers twitched in their last futile flutterings, watched till her wide-open eyes clouded at last in death.

Then, carefully, he wiped the knife on the already stained shirt, packed both into the doctor's bag with the rest of his instruments and snapped the lock shut.

Stepping carefully over the body he moved to the bedroom door, listening for signs of entry.

But there was nothing.

From there he crossed to the window and glanced out.

The top of Officer Potter's helmet still moved backwards and forwards outside the back gate.

Satisfied, he came back to stand over Nancy's corpse.

He knelt down and, as a doctor might, he closed the dead woman's eyelids.

The action brought him back to himself.

He was no longer a doctor.

He was Edward Hyde.

Stuck in a house with a dead body.

God in heaven. How was he going to reclaim his *alter ego,* Jekyll? He was miles from home, from his potion, from safety. Police were guarding Jekyll's house. Guarding this house too. He was a wanted man.

He began to shake with terror. He didn't want to die. He had only just begun to live.

Wait a minute. Calm. Calm. He forced himself to get a grip on his mind.

If he could will himself to become Hyde, why not the other way round?

He closed his eyes and tried to think good thoughts, to draw Jekyll out.

But it was useless. For whereas Jekyll had some bad in him, Hyde was pure evil, had not one single ounce of decency in his makeup, did not know what a good thought felt like.

Panic seized him.

He pushed it aside. Calm. Calm. Don't get excited. The police have no evidence. Their star witness is dead.

Yes. And you killed her. And if they find you here . . .

But where can I go?

Calm. Calm.

Sit down. Think.

He made himself sit on the bed, to stop his fractured thoughts chasing their own tails in his head.

What he needed was a plan.

What he needed was a place to hide.

A place for Hyde to hide. For Hyde to hide. For Hyde to hide.

Stop!

He held his head to stop the jangling. To force his mind to focus.

A place to hide.

Somewhere where the police would never think of looking for him.

Where?

What he needed was someone to bring the powders to him.

Who?

Whom could he trust?

No one.

Hyde hadn't a friend in the world.

Jekyll then. Whom could Jekyll trust?

Mary.

Of course, Mary.

He would be safe in Mary's house. Safe until she brought the powders to him. She would do it for Jekyll.

He stared out of the window at the winter sky.

The nights were drawing in early.

All he had to do was sit tight till dark.

Sit tight and hope that the police didn't check on Nancy.

If his luck held, then he could creep out under cover of night and pay a visit to the lovely Mary Carew.

ELEVEN

Mary Carew had been weeping most of the day. [H]
green eyes were red-rimmed and her hair tousled [a]
untidy.

But even in grief she managed to retain a semblanc[e]
dignity.

When Richard Enfield presented himself at her d[oor]
she dismissed the snivelling chambermaid and ca[me]
forward to greet him with hands outstretched.

Not until he began to offer his stammering con[do]
lences did she break down, crumpling against his c[hest]
in a flood of tears.

Enfield folded his arms around her and murmu[red]
into her hair, words of comfort and endearment.

Mary would have been glad to stay that way ind[efi]
nitely, secure in the warmth of her cousin's affecti[on]
but she could not allow herself to be so self-indulg[ent]
After a few moments she pushed herself away, borr[ow]
ing Enfield's handkerchief to dry her eyes.

"Forgive me for being so silly," she apologiz[ed]
blowing her nose in a businesslike manner, "but it's b[een]
a truly dreadful day. What with poor Father . . ." H[ere]
she almost broke down again and Enfield stepped [to]
wards her, but she raised a hand to stop him, pul[led]
herself together and carried on. "All the arrangeme[nts]
for the wedding having to be cancelled . . . and He[nry]
. . . Henry disappearing into thin air."

"They still have not located him, then?"

Mary shook her head.

"Now, when I need him most, he simply cannot be found. You don't know where he is, do you, Richard?"

"I'm sorry, my dear. I fear I have no idea."

"There was one terrible point at the beginning of the day when they thought Henry had killed Father. I fancied I should go mad then. But now, thank goodness, they have transferred their attention to someone else."

"Hyde," said Enfield through clenched teeth. "Edward Hyde."

"You know him?"

"Unfortunately."

"Who is he? Why should he do such a dreadful thing?"

"He is a fiend in human form. A degenerate. A sadist. Why he should want to . . . I have no idea. But I doubt he would need a motive. The man is vile."

* * *

On the sill outside that first-floor window, Hyde ground his pointed teeth.

It was all he needed.

As though he hadn't had enough trouble getting here, what with almost being caught on his way out . . .

And now to arrive and find this prating dandy paying court to Mary Carew under the pretense of offering sympathy. He might fool Mary. He might fool Jekyll. But he didn't fool Hyde—not for one moment.

He began to chew ferociously at his nails. His nerves were stretched to breaking point. It did not suit him to be on the run. Like every bully he was a coward and his near apprehension by the police had left him in a state of extreme agitation.

He was sure he had judged it nicely, waiting till dusk fell over Soho before opening the bedroom window to sneak out and away.

But his luck had deserted him.

Officer Arnold had let himself in through the front door just as Hyde was sliding out into the back yard.

He shuddered to remember what came next. The policeman's startled oath as he tripped over Nancy's body. The sound of him flailing around in the dark. The creak of the gate at the bottom of the yard.

Hyde had just managed to fling himself over the wall into the next yard before the policeman had thrust his head out of the window, shouting for Officer Potter, who came thundering through the gate, colliding with the bathtub and sending gin bottles crashing in all directions.

The noise had brought the neighbors to their back door, throwing a band of light out onto Hyde's prone figure.

Fear had galvanized him into action.

He had leaped up onto the top of an old shed and fled over the rooftops with the shrill sound of whistles ringing in his ears.

Only his superior strength and unnatural agility had kept him ahead of the law, allowing him to leap distances between buildings that no sane man would have even attempted.

At last, when his breath had seemed about to fail, the sounds of pursuit had died away and he had swung down from the top of the factory building where he was hiding, to skulk the rest of the way to the Carew home among the shadows of dim alleys and the comparative safety of night-quiet gardens.

And now he had arrived to find the object of his quest being entertained by some moon-faced buffoon with nothing better to do than try to steal another man's fiancée when he was out of the way.

He grimaced with impatience and frustration.

When would the fool go?

As if in answer to his question, Enfield pressed Mary's hand to his lips and made to leave her.

She stood on tiptoe to kiss him on the cheek and Hyde—watching through the window—felt the pangs of jealousy tear at him.

"Thank you for coming, Richard," she said. "You will tell me at once if you hear anything of Henry?"

"Of course, my dear," Enfield assured her.

"I can't understand it. He must have heard the news by now. Yet still he does not come. It is so unlike him."

Enfield murmured something else which Hyde could not catch, and then, with a click of his heels, he was gone.

* * *

Mary closed the door behind him.

Dear Richard. He was such a comfort. She knew how fond he was of her. But she could not think of that now. Her throughts were all for Henry. And her poor dead father.

Tears welled in her eyes.

This was to have been such a happy day. Her wedding day. Oh, where was Henry? Where?

She sank onto the stool in front of her dressing-table and buried her face in her hands.

There was a sudden clicking sound, as of a catch being undone.

She raised her head, expecting to see Dobbs, her maid, entering the room. It would not do to be seen in such a state in front of the girl. She was already upset enough.

Someone—no, something—was climbing in through the window. Mary could see its reflection in the mirror as it scrambled over the sill.

Her heart lurched in terror and her hand flew to her throat.

"Don't move," said the thing. The voice, cruel and hard, brooked no disobedience. "Don't cry out. Unless you want Henry Jekyll dead."

Mary despised the kind of woman who was forever fainting at the least little thing. She had always prided herself on her courage.

But pride goeth before destruction, and Mary's courage all but deserted her in the face of the misshapen creature that had crawled into her bedroom out of the blackness of the night.

Turning unsteadily on her stool, she faced the intruder with what little remained of her self-control.

"Who are you?" she said, her voice unnaturally high and cracking under the strain. "What do you want?"

The creature came closer, leaning over her until she could feel its hot breath on her face, smell the fear oozing from its pores to mingle with her own. The eyes bored into her, fearful, frightening eyes, hard and cruel with a hint of madness.

"I am Edward Hyde," it said.

Mary cringed away.

This was her father's murderer.

Had he come to murder her too?

"Why?" she said. "What did we ever do to you?"

"Shut up," snapped the monster. "And don't move. Unless you want to taste death right now."

Mary sat stock still.

"I have your fiancé," continued Hyde. "Unless you do as I ask you will never see him again."

Mary felt something like relief.

It wasn't Henry's fault. He would have come to her if he could. This monster had him imprisoned, locked away somewhere. His life was in her hands.

She did not hesitate.

"I will do anything you ask," she said.

"I need some drugs," said Hyde. "I *must* have them. Now. As soon as possible. They are in Jekyll's house."

* * *

Outside the door, Dobbs paused with her hand raised to knock.

Someone was with the mistress.

Who?

Mr. Enfield had left. She had let him out herself. And no one had come in—at least not by the front door.

Gingerly she knelt and applied her eye to the keyhole.

The face that swam into her vision was like every nightmare she had ever known—and worse.

Dobbs had had a disturbing day.

The face was the last straw.

She leapt to her feet and hurtled down the stairs, screeching her lungs out.

"Help . . . Murder . . . Police."

The young police officer, who had been given express instructions not to move from the house, came tearing up from the kitchen with a piece of Cook's best pork pie clutched in one hand.

He barged into Mary Carew's bedroom just in time to see Hyde crash through the window and out into the night.

* * *

Hyde landed heavily on the soft grass, twisting his ankle.

He struggled to his feet and limped away into the darkness.

Again the whistles.

Again the sounds of pursuit.

But this time he could not run, could not climb. His ankle pained him too much.

He stumbled into the main road and was almost knocked down by a passing cab.

"Ere. Watch where you're going, can't you?" the cabby shouted.

"Hold your noise." Hyde yelled back.

Pulling his cloak up around his face, he scrambled aboard the empty cab and issued his instructions.

"Pieces of Eight. Grafton Street . . . and hurry."

"Drunks," muttered the cabby and, clicking his reins to encourage his horse into a trot, set off in the direction of the docks.

* * *

By the time the eager young policeman arrived in the street the cab had rounded the corner, taking the elusive Mr. Hyde with it.

TWELVE

The Pieces of Eight was a disreputable inn haunted by disreputable people.

It was a place where one could buy anything—even silence—provided one had enough money to pay for it.

The landlord, Jay Higgins, was a big, greasy lard-barrel of a man noted for his singular lack of morals.

But his soft exterior held an iron core. Higgins had broken more heads in his time than he had worn clean shirts.

Higgins feared nothing and no one.

Except perhaps for the man who now stood just inside the door of the small room.

Swathed in an opera cloak, the hood pulled up over his head, it was impossible to distinguish his features. But Higgins recognized the nervous, darting movements of the man.

Hyde had been a good customer in his time.

It had been Higgins's dubious privilege to act as go-between in many arrangements to satisfy Hyde's monumental appetite for depravity.

And now the man was wanted all over London—for murder.

Big reward for him too.

Well, he was not the first murderer Higgins had encountered, nor would he be the last.

"Take over the bar, Elsie," he said to the buxom girl clearing tables. "I gotta bitta business to do."

* * *

93

Higgins led Hyde up the rickety stairs that he had climbed so many times before in search of questionable pleasures.

Floorboards creaked and the sound of giggling and coarse voices filtered from the rooms as they passed.

The landlord stopped finally at the last door at the end of a dingy corridor and, selecting a key from the heavy ring that hung from his belt, let his customer into the uninviting room.

"You'll be safe here," he said.

Hyde fixed him with a cold stare.

"I'd better be," he answered.

Higgins felt something stir deep in the pit of his stomach. Revulsion? Hardly. He had seen things in his time . . . Fear, then? Not that either . . . more queasiness crossed with a grudging respect. This was a man even he would think twice about crossing . . . despite the sizeable reward being offered for his capture.

"I have some letters to write," said Hyde. "I'll need a pen and some paper . . . and a lad to deliver them when they're done."

"It'll cost you."

"Name your price."

This was music to Higgins's ears.

"Twenty pounds," he said, "for the paper. Fifty for the room. A half-crown for the boy to take 'em."

"Highway robbery," objected Hyde.

"Take it or leave it."

"I'll take it," said the fugitive, then shook his head at the landlord's outstretched palm. "*After* the letters have been delivered."

* * *

The bargain struck, Higgins brought the paper, pen and ink and left Hyde to his own devices.

Never had Hyde's brain felt so sharp. Necessity, in truth, was the mother of invention, and he had spent the whole of his carriage trip to the inn inventing a plan to replace the one which lay in tatters in Mary Carew's bedroom.

It was fortunate that in the guise of Hyde he retained one feature which was purely Jekyll's—his handwriting.

Accordingly, the first letter he wrote was to his old friend Lanyon.

Lanyon, the unbeliever. He would show Lanyon, he thought, convince him of the truth of what he had said at the dinner party and extricate himself from a deep hole at the same time.

Kill two birds with one stone.

The letter read thus:

My dear Lanyon,

If our previous friendship ever meant anything to you, I beg you to do me one favor now.

Believe me when I assure you that it is a matter of life and death.

Go to my house, I beseech you, and collect from there some powders and a solution which are to be found in the third drawer down in a small chest in my laboratory.

Poole will be expecting you and has been instructed to lend you every assistance.

Take the complete drawer back to your own apartment and there await the arrival of a visitor who will call on you at midnight.

Do not fail me in this, Lanyon. I cannot impress on you too strongly the urgency of the matter.

Be assured that this is the last service I will ever ask of you. Tell no one.

* * *

He signed it "Your erstwhile and still affectionate friend, Henry Jekyll."

The other letter, written to Poole, told the butler to expect Lanyon's arrival, allow him access to the laboratory and permit him to remove the drawer.

The letters written, Hyde called for Higgins and ordered him to have them delivered post haste. Only when the boy returned with assurances that they had safely reached their destinations would the promised money be forthcoming.

"And Higgins," he added softly, clasping the landlord's sleeve as the big man turned to leave. "Do not betray me. I am a desperate man. And desperate men do desperate deeds."

And Higgins, recognizing in that depraved countenance something even more corrupt and unscrupulous than himself, set aside any thought of the thousand pound reward, and did as he was bid.

THIRTEEN

Lanyon thought long and hard before yielding to Henry Jekyll's request. He was a man who held a grudge and, in truth, he wanted nothing more to do with his former friend.

But he could not deny the obvious note of desperation in the letter and finally, against his better judgment, he called for his carriage and set off on his strange errand.

Poole was waiting nervously for him in the hall of the big house. He did not greet the doctor or even offer to take his coat, but instead led him directly through the building and up the stairs to Jekyll's laboratory.

Lanyon liked order and punctuality in his life. He cherished the familiar, detested the unusual. His temper was not improved by the butler's uncharacteristic behavior.

"Any idea what this is about, Poole?" he asked testily.

"None, sir." The butler was stony-faced. "I was hoping you might be able to tell me. The master has been missing since last evening and we are all very concerned."

"I shouldn't bother your heads about him. He'll be back when the mood takes him, no doubt."

"As you say, sir."

"Really, the man has no regard for the feelings of others. You'd think, with his father-in-law newly murdered, he'd have better things to do with his time than play games."

Poole declined to comment. He merely pointed out the relevant drawer and handed over the key.

Lanyon unlocked it and eased it out, inspecting the contents. They seemed innocent enough. Some two dozen or so packets of powders, a vial of crimson liquid and a black experiment notebook bearing the inscription "J-H Experiments".

He flicked through the book. It was marked in some kind of code. A puzzling collection of capitals interspersed with an occasional words such as "Daisy" meant nothing to him.

He unwrapped one of the screws of paper. Inside was a quantity of white powder. He dipped a finger in and licked it experimentally. The taste told him nothing other than that it was an innocuous mixture of mineral salts.

"Is this all?" he asked crossly.

"It would appear so, sir."

"I can't imagine what's so important about this lot to make a man come right across town and miss his dinner."

"Would you care for a basket, sir?" enquired Poole, not wishing to be drawn into an argument.

"No, no. The letter said I should bring the whole drawer. Can't think why. Bring me a sheet, will you, to wrap the damn thing in?"

"Perhaps a pillowcase, sir?"

"Whatever. Just bring me something and let's be done with it. I've had a hard day and I'm heartily sick of the whole affair."

The butler brought the pillowcase and held it wide while Lanyon slotted the drawer into its mouth as one might slot a letter into an envelope. Then, together the

wo men carried the unwieldy package downstairs and
aid it in Lanyon's carriage. Lanyon climbed in beside it.

"You will let me know, sir," said Poole anxiously, "if
ou have any word of Dr. Jekyll?"

"You may be sure of it, Poole," said Lanyon grimly.
Expect him home sometime after midnight with his
ail between his legs."

Then, with a sharp rap of his cane, he ordered his
oachman home.

It was past ten o'clock by the time he arrived.

He took the drawer directly to his study on the first
loor. Having checked that the contents were still intact,
e hurried down to the dining room where his disgrun-
led cook served him cold mutton, lumpy dumplings
nd soggy cabbage swimming in congealing gravy. He
te too fast, swilling the meal down with a bottle of port
nd following the main course with double helpings of
uet pudding and brandy sauce.

The inevitable indigestion which followed seemed
vorse than usual and did nothing to ease his ill-temper.
When, by five minutes past midnight, his expected
visitor" had still not arrived, he was angry enough to
hrow the drawer out into the street.

He retired to his study and was pouring himself a
hird "medicinal" port in an attempt to settle his
tomach when he heard first the police whistles and
hen, hard on their heels, the sound of someone ham-
nering his front door.

He went to the window, drew aside the curtains and
oked down into the shadowy street.

A police van was drawn up at the end of the road and
everal policemen were moving among the houses clear-
y searching for something—or someone.

Behind him, Lanyon heard the door open and a voice announcing: "A visitor for you, sir."

He turned to face his manservant and a dark, hooded figure.

"He will not give his name, sir."

Lanyon waved dismissively.

"That will be all, Jenkins," he said.

The figure stayed where it was, motionless, until Jenkins had retired, closing the door behind him.

Only then did it speak.

"You have the drawer?" it said.

Lanyon had long suspected that his "visitor" would be none other than Jekyll himself, but now he realized that he had been mistaken. Not only was the figure much shorter than Jekyll, but the voice, echoing from the dark depths of the opera cloak, was definitely not that of his colleague. Henry, he had grudgingly to admit, had a most pleasant, soothing voice, unlike this one, which was chilling, almost inhuman in quality.

Lanyon began to feel decidedly uncomfortable. He moved towards his desk to be closer to the revolver that lay in the top drawer.

"Who are you, sir?" he demanded. "What do you mean, visiting my home at this hour?"

"Don't try to bluff me, Lanyon." The voice was harsh and tinged with more than a hint of desperation. "I have come for the drawer. Do you have it?"

"I warn you," said Lanyon. "The police are outside . . ."

The figure hurried to the window and raised the edge of the curtain. Lanyon noticed that he walked with a slight limp. He peered out into the rain-dark night for a moment and then, apparently content with what he saw dropped the curtain and turned to face the doctor once more.

"They have moved on," he said smugly.

"I was . . . I was expecting someone else," said Lanyon, moving closer to the revolver, playing for time.

"You were expecting Jekyll," said the figure. "And you will see him soon enough. Only give me what you brought from his house."

"I cannot do that," said Lanyon, easing out the drawer of his desk and curling his hand around the butt of the small weapon that lay inside, "unless I have written authority from Jekyll instructing me to do so."

The creature was on him before he knew what was happening. It launched itself across the room like an unexpected bolt of lightning, knocking him backwards and wrestling the gun from his hands.

Without really knowing how it had happened, Lanyon found himself flat on his back, staring down the barrel of his own revolver.

"Enough of these games," said the figure. "Get me the drawer. Now."

"It is in the corner," gasped Lanyon. "On the small table, wrapped in a pillowcase."

"That's better," said the visitor. He waved the muzzle of the gun under Lanyon's nose. "Get up. And just in case you should be feeling heroic, remember this. I am a crack shot. Should you attempt to pull the bell to summon help, or should you utter a sound, one tiny sound, without my permission, I shall not hesitate to shoot you right beteen the eyes."

Lanyon recognized the veracity of the statement. For the first time in his life he felt real fear. He was closeted in his own home with a murderer. If he had been in unfamiliar surroundings it would have been bad enough. But that the nightmare should be happening here, in his own study, seemed to make the whole thing much worse.

He clambered unsteadily to his feet.

"Very good," said the figure. "Now stay there. And don't move."

"May I sit down?" stammered Lanyon. "I don't feel very well."

The figure chuckled.

"I should if I were you. If you are feeling ill now, let me assure you, you will be more so before this evening's events are over."

Lanyon sat down groggily in his chair. The figure moved to the corner, removed the drawer from the pillowcase and examined the contents closely for a moment or two.

Satisfied, he moved back to the desk and stood facing his discomfited host.

"You are a privileged man," he said. "You are about to witness something which no one has ever seen before. You are about to become privy to one of the world's greatest experiments."

If Lanyon had not known better, he would have said that this was Henry Jekyll speaking. The phraseology was his. The fanaticism. Only the voice was different.

"You know to what I refer," the voice continued. "I mean the experiment to separate good and evil."

Lanyon could not see the face properly but, from beneath the shadow of the hood, two eyes glittered dangerously at him. The creature was clearly mad. Jekyll had filled its brain with his outlandish theories and turned its head.

"But first," said the figure, "you must know whom I am."

It threw aside the hood.

Lanyon felt his heart lurch in his chest.

The creature smiled at him, a horrible mirthless smile.

"You recognize me, then?" it smirked.

Recognize him? How could he not recognize him, Lanyon wondered. Those evil features had been emblazoned on the front page of every newspaper in London.

This was the infamous Edward Hyde. Murderer of Sir Danvers Carew. So that was what the police had been doing in the street.

If only he could get to the window, summon help.

"Don't even think of it," said Hyde, as though reading his mind. "It will be the last move you will ever make."

A strange, tingling sensation began to take hold in Lanyon's arm. His hand felt suddenly numb. He looked down at it. It was deathly pale, as if all the blood had been drained from it.

"Unbeliever," sneered Hyde. "Doubting Thomas. You, who scorned the theories of your betters, you are to be so honored as to be the first human being—alive—to view the fruits of Jekyll's experiments."

Taking a tall glass from the drinks tray, Hyde moved back to the drawer. Then, holding the glass aloft, he emptied into it the contents of one of the paper envelopes. This done, he unstoppered the vial and added a number of drops of the red solution.

The resulting mixture foamed and fizzed, turned purple and finally, as the effervescence died away, a pale, almost luminous green.

Lanyon felt distinctly unwell. The pins and needles were tingling right up to his shoulder now.

103

Hyde held the mixture up in front of his face and gazed longingly into its depths.

"Observe," he said.

Then, in one enormous gulp, he swallowed the potion down.

What happened next was terrible to see.

Hyde began to clutch at his throat and gasp for breath. His eyes started to bulge, his tongue to loll from his mouth. His face turned a deep, mottled red. Clearly the man was in agony.

Then, as if that weren't enough, the very fabric of his body began to alter, the bones heaving under the skin, like a baby turning in its mother's womb.

Before Lanyon's horrified gaze, the face and neck began to lengthen, the ape-like arms to shrink. The teeth in the gappy mouth began to straighten and grow together, the hair and eyes to lighten. The bowed stance changed to a more upright posture.

"No, no," cried Lanyon, raising trembling hands to cover his unbelieving eyes.

"Look, Lanyon, look," cried Jekyll.

Because it was now *almost* Jekyll who stood before him, Jekyll's voice that denied him the right to look away, Jekyll's blue eyes that stared out of the horrible hybrid face. Half man. Half monster.

Lanyon struggled to his feet. The tingling in his arm had turned to pain. It seared in stabbing thrusts up towards his shoulder, from where it fanned out into his chest. He held onto the edge of the desk for support. Lights began to dance in front of his eyes.

"Lanyon." Jekyll's voice swam at him through the murk. He felt strong arms holding his shoulders, supporting him.

"Lanyon." The voice was filled with the concern of

years of friendship. "Sit down, old man," it said. "You don't look at all well."

The mist cleared from Lanyon's eyes. He found himself staring into the face of Dr. Henry Jekyll. Pure. Unadulterated. The kind, caring face of this man who would be God.

"Foul fiend," croaked Lanyon. "Blasphemer. You are in league with the devil."

He shrugged Jekyll's hands away and staggered to the corner of the room. Clasping the drawer in both hands he hurled it, with the last of his strength, contents and all, into the fire.

"Nooooooo." Jekyll's cry was that of a lost soul.

But Lanyon scarcely heard it.

The huge, driving surge of pain that filled his chest took up all his attention. It was his heart. He knew that now. His heart. Bursting under the strain.

His last sight, before the blackness of death engulfed him, was of his old college companion, on his hands and knees before the fire, scrabbling among the glowing embers like some satanic disciple at the gateway to hell.

FOURTEEN

When Enfield arrived next morning with Mary Carew on his arm, Jekyll was at breakfast. He invited his friend and fiancée to join him in some eggs and a slice of ham.

"I don't know how you can think of food," said the distraught Mary. "Where have you been for the past thirty-six hours, Henry? We have been half mad with worry."

"I have been walking," said Jekyll.

"Walking?" spluttered Enfield. "Walking? Where?"

"Just walking," said Henry vaguely. "I needed to get away—to think."

"But we thought . . ." began Mary.

Enfield finished the sentence for her.

"We thought you'd been kidnapped by that madman, Hyde."

Jekyll looked astonished.

"Kidnapped—whatever gave you that impression?"

"Because . . . because he broke into my room . . ." said Mary haltingly. She stopped, too overcome to continue.

Enfield put a protective arm around her shoulder.

"He broke into her room and almost scared her half to death . . . said if she wanted to see you again she'd better get him some drug or other. If there hadn't been a policeman on the premises, heaven only knows what might have happened."

Jekyll got to his feet and laid his napkin carefully beside his plate.

"Oh my dear," he said. "How terrible for you."

He held out his arms and, much to Enfield's chagrin, Mary rushed across the room and flung herself into his embrace.

Jekyll began to stroke her hair, murmuring soothing phrases while his eyes locked onto Enfield's in a way that left him in no doubt who was in control of the situation.

"You owe us an explanation, Jekyll," said Enfield stiffly. "During the time you were away Hyde has committed two murders and broken into your fiancée's bedroom. Where have you been, man? I should have thought your place was with Mary."

Mary raised her head and looked at Jekyll with pleading eyes.

"Richard is right, Henry," she said. "Where were you when I needed you?"

"I told you, my dear. I was walking."

"In the name of heaven, Jekyll," thundered Enfield, "we deserve more explanation than that. Utterson and I have had the police on our backs for twenty-four hours. Mary has been attacked, had her father most cruelly taken from her and her wedding cancelled. We hear nothing from you for thirty-six hours. We assume you kidnapped, perhaps foully murdered. And now we arrive to find you coolly eating breakfast and you tell us you were out walking? It simply won't do, man. It simply will not do."

"I'm afraid it will have to do," said Jekyll. "There is no more."

"Then why didn't you send word, Henry?" said Mary, feeling a little foolish now that Henry was safely back. "You must have known I would be upset."

"I could not face you, my love," said Jekyll. "Can you understand that and forgive me?"

Enfield snorted.

Evidently *he* could not.

"Let me explain," said Jekyll gently, taking Mary's hands and gazing earnestly into her eyes. "On the night of . . . of your father's death, I was called to a breech birth. It was a long, hard delivery, but fortunately successful. The house was a poor one in the East End but the new birth (it was a fine boy) filled the humble surroundings with hope. The family insisted I share their frugal breakfast."

"Then you did not know that my father . . . ?"

"I did not. I left the house sometime after eleven A.M. It was my wedding day. I was happy. And, since it was a glorious morning and the action of bringing a new life into the world always elates me, I decided to walk home."

"Then why didn't you?" muttered Enfield.

"Because, my dear Richard, halfway up the Strand I came face to face with a newsboy."

"All the more reason, I should have thought, to come straight back."

"On the contrary. Bear with me, Richard, Mary, while I try to explain my reaction to the brutal story that confronted me. I was overcome first with disbelief, then with horror, guilt, fear. I felt responsible for the whole ghastly business."

"And Mary? What of her?" exploded Enfield. "Deprived of her father and her husband-to-be in one fell swoop?"

"It was because of Mary that I did not come home. I knew what she must be suffering but the remorse . . . the shame . . . that a friend of mine . . . I felt my presence would only serve to remind her that it was a friend of mine . . . I felt she might reject me. That someone of my acquaintance should perpetrate such a foul act . . . My one excuse is that I temporarily lost my wits. I began to walk . . ."

"Where did you go, Henry?" asked Mary, begging to be convinced, reassured, in the face of Enfield's scepticism.

"I know not, my darling, only that I walked, aimlessly, my thoughts in a turmoil, my whole future, which until then seemed so safe, so assured, turned upside down."

"Poor Henry."

"Poor Henry," snorted Enfield. "You are easily persuaded, cousin. Ask him why, when he eventually came to his senses, he did not rush to your side? Why we had to hear from Poole that he had returned? Why, when we came to confront him, we found him calmly partaking of ham as though nothing had happened?"

"I know it must seem strange," conceded Jekyll. "But I will be frank. On my wanderings I visited various taverns and drank more ale than was good for me in an attempt to blot out the awful truth. At one point I fell and twisted my ankle." Here he exhibited a bandaged foot. "When at last I found my way home in the early hours of this morning, I was in no fit state to receive anyone. Poole, very sensibly, put me to bed."

"That's still no reason . . ." began Enfield, but Jekyll raised a hand to silence him.

"I was roused from my bed at seven-thirty by one Chief Inspector Watson. He kept me fairly busy answering questions for an hour and a half. When he left, I found that I was ravenous. I had called for my carriage and was about to leave for Mary's house when you anticipated me by arriving here."

"Why did the chief inspector keep you for so long?" Mary wanted to know.

"He had some foolish notion that I might know the whereabouts of Edward Hyde. I could not at first persuade him to the contary."

"Then why didn't he take you to the police station?" asked Enfield. "I would have done, if I had been the chief inspector and you told me you'd spent twenty-four hours 'walking'."

"I was able to clear myself by showing him a letter. It was pushed under the door of my laboratory sometime during the night. Perhaps you would care to read it?"

Jekyll felt in the pocket of his silk dressing-gown, produced a folded piece of paper and handed it to Enfield.

"Read it aloud," he suggested, "so that Mary may hear."

Enfield cleared his throat.

"There is no address," he began, "and the writing is scrawled as if it had been written in a hurry."

"Never mind that, Richard," said Mary impatiently. "What does it say?"

"It says, 'My dear Jekyll, I am going away. Somewhere where no one can find me. Neither you, nor anyone close to you, will ever see me again. I freely confess to the murder of both Sir Danvers Carew and the woman known as Nancy. My confession is not made out of remorse. I have no regrets—but to exonerate you from any suspicion or blame. You, Jekyll, of all the people in the world, have been my only true friend. I send my warmest regards and sincere regrets for any inconvenience caused . . .'" Inconvenience. He calls murder . . . inconvenience."

"Please continue, Richard," said Mary.

"That is all . . . it just says . . . 'I remain, your affectionate and loyal friend, Edward Hyde'."

"Mr. Utterson, sir."

Poole's modulated tones ushered the lawyer into the breakfast room.

At the sight of Jekyll, he strode across to the younger man and began to pump his hand vigorously.

"Henry," he said. "Thank God."

If anything, Utterson looked more woebegone than usual. His sad, bloodhound face seemed to have lengthened to the point where the lantern jaw almost brushed his chest. His eyes were puffy from lack of sleep.

"Good lord, John," said Jekyll, putting a solicitous hand on his friend's shoulder. "You look frightful."

"As well I might," said Utterson. He sat down and mopped his brow with a voluminous handkerchief. "Oh my, what a series of disasters."

The blood drained from Mary Carew's face. She clutched Jekyll's sleeve. Her courage seemed to have quite deserted her.

"Merciful heavens," she said, "what now?"

"It is Lanyon," said Utterson, in sepulchral tones. "He suffered heart failure during the night, not long after receiving a mysterious visitor. He is dead."

For one dreadful moment it looked as though Henry Jekyll was going to laugh. Certainly a fleeting grin crossed his features and for a moment a very strange look took possession of his eyes. He raised his hand to his throat and a dark, mottled flush tinged his jowls.

"No," he muttered. "Get back."

"Henry." Mary put a hand to his cheek. "Whatever's the matter?"

"Go away," said Jekyll, brushing her hand aside roughly.

"What?"

"Go away," shouted Jekyll, his expression changing to one of malice. "You must all go away. Now."

Utterson stood up.

"Come now, Henry," he said soothingly. "I know this has been a shock . . ."

"Get out," shouted Jekyll. "All of you. Leave, do you hear?"

"Now look here, Jekyll," said Enfield furiously.

"Well, if you won't go, then I must," yelled Jekyll.

He shoved Mary aside and, pushing roughly past the two men, hurled himself into the hall.

Utterson, Enfield and Mary listened, dumbfounded, to the sound of his feet thumping up the laboratory stairs, followed by an ear-splitting crash as he slammed the door and turned the key in the lock.

There was a stunned silence.

And then, across the house, like church bells wafted on a summer breeze, came the sound of someone laughing.

It was a sound that froze the blood.

Utterson shook his head.

"Poor Henry," he said. "It has all been too much for him. He has taken leave of his senses."

Mary lowered her head, her shoulders heaving silently, trying to hide her misery, and failing.

Enfield thrust the letter into Utterson's hand and crossed the room to comfort her.

"Come away, my dear," he said. "This is no place for you."

"But . . . he might need me . . ." she said chokingly.

"What he needs is a doctor," said Enfield. "We will arrange it."

"Physician, heal thyself," intoned Utterson, scanning the letter. Then he frowned. "That's strange," he said.

"What?"

"This letter. From Hyde. The writing's different, of course, but some of the capitals . . ."

"Yes?"

"Some of the capitals—the A and the R, for instance —are formed just the same way that Henry forms his."

"You're not suggesting . . ." Mary was outraged. "You're not suggesting that Henry wrote it himself?"

Utterson cocked his head to listen.

The laughter had died away to a chuckle. It echoed round the house, inanely, insanely.

The lawyer looked directly at Mary.

"Quite frankly, my dear," he said, "I don't know what to think."

FIFTEEN

Hyde paced the laboratory, muttering to himself—and laughing.

Laughing at Utterson, that pompous ass, and Lanyon, that self-opinionated bore, pop-eyed and apopleptic to the last, and Enfield, that strutting simpleton, and Mary—taken in by his posturing, pretending love for Jekyll but ready to fall into her cousins's arms if things became too difficult.

Hypocrites.

Self-deluding imbeciles.

Only he could see the truth. He. Hyde.

And the truth was that man was an animal at heart, hiding his bestiality under a cloak of fine manners.

And Hyde was the greatest animal of them all. He was supreme. Because he recognized reality.

Might was right.

He was the master of them all.

He stopped his pacing, began to chew his nail.

And yet he could not go out, could not exercise his power except in the guise of Henry Jekyll. And Jekyll was too weak to take advantage of it.

Well, that was easily solved. He had more power than Jekyll now, was more than his match. He could use him to appear and disappear at will.

He could supplant Jekyll.

But Jekyll did not have the strength to supplant him.

Hyde held the ultimate power.

Jekyll was his tool, his plaything.

And now it was time to bring Jekyll back for awhile. Hyde needed him. He went to the chest of drawers and took, from the second drawer where he had secreted them the night before, the items that he had managed to snatch from the fire.

The area where the third drawer should have been now gaped like an open wound, the drawer itself having perished in the flames.

The memory made Hyde seethe.

That idiot Lanyon. He might have ruined everything —almost had.

Hyde laid the items on the table. The experiment book, badly charred at the edges, the vial of solution, its glass dented and warped where it had almost melted in the heat, and two powders, all that was left of his considerable store.

The inconvenience of it irritated him.

Now he must get more.

He would send Poole for them.

But first he must transform his features back into the more acceptable face of Henry Jekyll.

He took a beaker from one of the shelves and began to mix the potion, opening the last but one of those precious powders.

* * *

Downstairs, Enfield had already left with Mary. Only Utterson had remained, to take Poole into his confidence.

"If there is no improvement by tomorrow, then I shall arrange for a physician to see him. Normally I would have called in Lanyon . . ." He let the sentence tail away into silence.

"Poor Dr. Lanyon," said Poole. "And him so young, too."

He did not mention the episode of the previous evening. Dr. Jekyll was in enough trouble already. Besides, Poole was not quite sure of his own legal standing in the matter. A mixture of loyalty and prudence caused him to hold his tongue.

"Should you get a chance to speak to him, Poole, ask him, will you, what he intends to do about Sir Danvers's funeral arrangements?"

"I'll do that, sir."

"If he feels unable to deal with them, then I suppose I shall have to tackle it myself. Can't expect Mary to handle it all alone."

"No, sir."

Poole handed Utterson his hat and cane.

The lawyer paused in the open doorway.

"Look after him, Poole," he said. "I would not have him harmed for all the world."

The butler's reply was drowned by the sound of the bell furiously summoning him to the laboratory.

He closed the door on Utterson's retreating back and hurried across the house and up the stairs.

Henry Jekyll stood in the doorway looking pale but composed. He held in his hand a note folded in four.

"Poole," he said, "I'd like you to have this prescription filled. Go to Macrae and Dickson."

"Yes, sir."

"At once, if you please. It is of the utmost importance."

"Of course, sir. I'll send Jarvis for it right away."

"No. Go yourself, Poole. I know I can trust you."

"As you wish, sir."

The butler turned to go and then, remembering Utterson's request, turned back.

"Beg pardon, sir."

"Yes, Poole?"

"Mr. Utterson asked me to ask whether you'd be making the funeral arrangements for Sir Danvers?"

For a moment Jekyll swayed in the doorway. He put out a hand to steady himself on the jamb. Suddenly he looked very tired.

"Ask Mr. Utterson if he would be kind enough to deal with that for me, please."

"Yes, sir."

"And Poole."

"Sir?"

"While we are discussing arrangements, cancel the wedding plans."

"They have already been postponed, sir."

"I know that, Poole. And now I want you to cancel them. Finally. Irrevocably. There will be no wedding. Not now. Not ever."

And he closed the door gently in the butler's astonished face.

* * *

Jekyll had decided that he could never marry Mary, must break with her entirely.

Not that he did not love her—he did—but every time he looked at her he would remember her father and that horrible night . . .

He shuddered.

Besides, he would have no time. He was determined that every waking hour would be devoted to his experiments. He must find a means to undo the wrong he had done—to bring his theories to their logical conclusion.

It was dreadful that things had gone so badly awry.

But he must not be discouraged. Every great man had had his failures. Once he had his new supply of powders, he could keep Hyde at bay, suppress him until he had the means to destroy him entirely.

He would kill the evil thing he had created . . .

"Noooooooo."

The scream rose to his throat unbidden.

Inside him, he felt the beast wake, rise to the surface, tearing its way upwards and outwards into the earth-light.

* * *

When Poole returned with the powders some half an hour later, Edward Hyde was once again supreme.

He dare not use the very last powder and so, since he also dare not be seen, he passed a note under the door instructing Poole to leave the package on the top step and retire.

The bemused butler did as he was bid, hurrying down to the servant's quarters to shake his head and click his tongue with Mrs. Johnson, the housekeeper.

When the coast was clear, Hyde retrieved the supplies and mixed the potion using one of the new powders.

It didn't work.

He tried another—with the same result.

Panic seized him.

Instead of throwing the ingredients together as he was wont to do, he measured them carefully into a graduated glass with all the meticulous accuracy that Henry Jekyll might have used.

Still no luck.

The mixture rocked and shook him as it normally did, but at the end of his rigors it was still Edward Hyde who stared back at him from the mirror.

Now he began to be afraid.

118

If the police should chance by and find him in this guise, he was done for.

He searched around for a reason why the potion was not working.

Perhaps he had grown used to the dosage and needed a larger measure? He mixed one, double the normal size.

The effects almost brought him to his knees, but the end result was the same.

No change.

At last Hyde hit upon the solution. The drug must be impure. Of course, that was it. The fools had given him an impure drug.

He felt his temper rising.

He would send Poole for more, with a note leaving Macrae and Dickson in no doubt as to what he thought of their incompetence.

He pulled the bell to summon the butler.

* * *

By nine o'clock that evening Hyde had mixed and swallowed twenty versions of the potion, concocted from powders brought from fifteen different chemists.

Each was recorded painstakingly in the experiment book.

Each had the same negative result.

Hyde was still Hyde.

He was also at his wits' end.

This was something he had not bargained for. His means of retreat was blocked. He was a sitting duck. Unable to escape. Unable to speak for fear the ever curious Poole should recognize Hyde's voice and call the police.

He had not eaten all day and the quantity of drugs he had taken had unhinged him, leaving him lightheaded and woolly-minded.

Now the chemists were all closed. He could get no more drugs till the morning.

Unless . . .

He rushed to the peg and unhooked his opera cape, slung it round his shoulders and clattered down the stairs to the back door.

He would break into the chemist, that was the answer. Macrae and Dickson's. They were the closest. The fools had probably given him the wrong thing in the first place. He would mix the powders himself. Then he would be sure of the right ingredients. You couldn't trust anyone else these days. If you wanted something done . . .

He felt in his pocket for the key.

The key.

My God—he had broken it.

He couldn't get out.

He was trapped.

Like an animal.

He sat down on the bottom step and began to howl.

* * *

The servants, hearing that eerie wailing, clung to each other and vowed that, come morning, they would leave this house of evil or know the reason why.

Only Poole kept a grip on himself. Not that he felt any more confident than the others. But the habits of a lifetime stood him in good stead.

He clapped his hands.

"That's enough," he said sharply. "We'll have no more of that talk, thank you very much. Dr. Jekyll has been a good and fair employer to you all. Now that he's going through a . . . spot of bother . . . I should have thought you'd have the Christian decency to stand by him. Instead you're behaving like a pack of rats, deserting a sinking ship."

The company in the kitchen looked suitably shame-faced.

"But the noise . . ." whimpered Elsie, the kitchen maid. "It's like a lost soul . . ."

"Don't be so fanciful, my girl," Poole reprimanded her.

The howling stopped.

"There," continued the butler. "It's over. Cook. Hot toddies to settle everyone's nerves, if you please. I am going to see if the doctor would like some supper."

"I should think he would," sniffed Cook, bustling off to the pantry to fetch the cooking brandy. "He hasn't eaten a bite all day."

* * *

Poole climbed the stairs into the main hall, showing more confidence than he felt.

He was worried about Dr. Jekyll. Very worried.

As soon as the other servants retired to bed, he intended to go to John Utterson's rooms and tell him of the doctor's strange behavior. The trips to the chemists. The quantities of drugs involved. The queer mutterings and cryings he'd heard through the laboratory door. The fact that Dr. Jekyll refused to see him . . . or even talk to him . . . and the howling . . . like a fiend in torment.

He reached the top stair and came into the hall.

A swirl of black caught his eye, heading for the front door.

"Hey," he shouted.

The cloaked figure turned to face him, the evil features drawn into a grimace of fear and rage.

"Keep back," it shrieked. "Keep back or I'll kill you."

Poole stepped back involuntarily, missing his footing and almost tumbling down the stairs. He reached out to grasp the banister, steadying himself.

"Don't come any closer," shouted the figure, fiddling with the catches of the front door.

Poole stood stock still.

It would take a braver man than him to tackle this madman, this murderer.

Without hindrance, Edward Hyde tore the front door wide and escaped out into the rain-soaked night.

* * *

Poole stood rooted to the spot.

Edward Hyde.

Here.

In the house.

With Dr. Jekyll.

Then where was the doctor now?

He hurried to the front door and forced it shut against the howling wind. Then, with an agility surprising in one of his age, he sprinted through to the laboratory stairs, climbed them two at a time and began to hammer on the locked door.

"Dr. Jekyll," he shouted. "Dr. Jekyll, are you there?"

Silence.

No voice answered his call.

Only the sighing of the trees in the teeth of the approaching storm broke the tomblike quiet of the house.

Poole sank to his knees in front of the door, applying his eye to the keyhole to see if he could catch a glimpse of his master. If he was hurt, ill, drugged.

But it was useless.

The interior of the room was black as a coal cellar.

A sudden bolt of lightning seared across the sky,

lighting up the windows and revealing the laboratory's secrets.

The room was in chaos, bottles, papers and glasses strewn higgledy-piggledy around the benches and floors.

But otherwise it was empty.

The lightning died and darkness descended once more.

And with the darkness the sudden realization came to Poole that his master must be dead.

Murdered by that evil creature he had apprehended in the hall.

That would account for the strange noises, the weird behavior. The last time he had seen Henry Jekyll had been that morning, when he had sent him for the first prescription. Had Hyde been with him then? In any case, he had certainly been with him when he came back.

Or was Jekyll already dead?

Poole was convinced now.

The doctor was dead—murdered by Hyde—and the body was hidden somewhere inside the locked room.

SIXTEEN

Hyde fled through the streets as though pursued by demons.

All his senses had been enhanced by the drugs, so that when the rain, driven by the rising wind, lashed his face it felt like small knives slicing his skin.

Fear drove him on—and a strange sense of exhilaration.

He was dicing with death—out here, in the streets, alone—with every man's hand against him and every policeman in London alerted to take him "dead or alive."

It was him against the world.

Well, he would give the world a run for its money.

He pounded on.

And the filthy weather stood him in good stead, for he reached Macrae and Dickson's without even seeing a policeman, let alone being challenged by one.

They were all back at the station house, he supposed, drinking mugs of tea, pretending concern for the welfare of the citizenry when all they were really concerned about was keeping their flat feet dry.

He darted into the doorway of the shop, peered through the window at the racks of doctor's jars temptingly displayed inside.

So near and yet so far.

He rattled the knob, twisted it, turned it, lost his temper and, exerting all his strength, tore it out of the wood and sent it hurtling through the stained glass of the door panel.

The noise was overlaid by a deep growl of thunder.

Using the following flash of lightning to his advantage, Hyde thrust his hand through the gaping hole in the glass, undid the bolts and swung the door wide.

Pushing behind the counter, he began to grab bottles at random, holding the labels squint-close in the half-light and then flinging them from him when they proved not to be what he was looking for.

He came upon one essential ingredient.

Then another.

But the third eluded him.

And all the time the pile of broken bottles and spilled salts mounted.

He cleared all the shelves, cursing with frustration.

The third element wasn't there.

Cramming the first two bottles in the pockets of his jacket, he crunched through the shards of broken glass and into the dispensary at the back of the shop.

He started rummaging through boxes and packages, creating havoc wherever he went. The first two elements were useless without the third. He poked and probed, tasted and tested, and all the while he shrieked and shouted till the noise of the storm could no longer conceal his rantings.

So immersed was he in the search that when the policeman's words cut through the dark he was taken completely by surprise.

"Hey," said the voice of the law. "What's going on in there?"

A shaft of light began to bob and weave through the shop. It paused at the pile of broken bottles behind the counter.

Dr. Jekyll and Mr. Hyde

"Suffering catfish," said the voice. "What a shambles."

Hyde crouched back against the door. He could see the beam of light approaching.

"Come on out now," ordered the officer. "I know you're in there."

The light traveled across the floor and then rose, wandering up the walls to shelf level where it paused . . . on the label of the missing ingredient.

With a howl of triumph, Hyde sprang from his hiding-place. He grabbed the bottle and then, nimble as a dancer, twirled on his toes and flung himself head first at his would-be captor.

The policeman took the blow full in the stomach.

He sat down with a startled grunt and Hyde trampled over him and out of the shop.

It took the policeman a good minute to get his breath back.

When he did, he put his whistle to his mouth and woke the whole neighborhood.

* * *

"He's murdered, sir, sure as eggs is eggs. And that fiend Hyde is the cause of it."

Utterson faced the distraught butler with all the composure he could muster.

"And you haven't seen Dr. Jekyll since this morning?"

"Not since just after you left, sir. Just notes and trips to the chemist. And more notes. And more trips."

"Most disturbing."

"And now, to come upon that monster in the middle of the hall. He's done for the master, sir, I know it."

"Contain yourself, Poole."

126

Utterson had never seen the man even ruffled before. Now he was so agitated that he could not stand still but kept hopping from foot to foot like a demented stork, twisting his handkerchief and wringing his hands.

"Please, Mr. Utterson, you must come, sir. I daren't go into that room alone and I don't want to call the police in case it's a false alarm."

"Of course I shall come," said the lawyer, shrugging into his raincoat. "But in the circumstances I feel it might be wise to stop and pick up Captain Enfield on the way."

* * *

Hyde reached home without any more trouble.

The forces of law and order took some time to muster, and when they did the winded officer had no idea in which direction the fugitive had fled.

Finding the front door bolted, Hyde smashed the dining-room window and climbed inside, heedless now of the noise he made or the commotion he created, desperate only to reach the laboratory, mix the drug, disappear.

He darted out into the hall and came upon Mrs. Johnson, a ghostly figure in a long white nightgown.

She took one look at him and began to scream.

Hyde felled her with a single blow, then bellowed belligerently into the darkness.

"Anybody else? Does anybody else wish to tackle Edward Hyde? I am here. In the house. Stay in your beds if you know what's good for you."

When no voice rose to challenge him he swirled round and, cape billowing behind him, headed for the stairs—and sanctuary.

He weighed and measured the powders in a frenzy,

then concocted the drug, hand trembling as he held the foaming glass till the liquid changed from red through purple to green.

He swallowed the mixture in great gulps, choking and coughing as it burned down his throat and into his system.

He staggered to the mirror as the pains racked him, holding on to the mantelpiece for support as his abused system rebelled against yet another onslaught from the malevolent drug.

He stared at his reflection . . . waiting . . .

But the face never wavered, the expression never changed.

Edward Hyde remained—stubbornly—Edward Hyde.

And suddenly Hyde was consumed with hatred for the image in the glass, for the sly, sensual features that had become his only face.

He raised one hairy fist and smashed it through the mirror, shattering it from top to bottom.

"Seven years bad luck," he yelled—and then he began to laugh. "If you live to see it out."

The laughter rose to a hysterical shriek and then changed, just as suddenly, to a despairing cry.

Hyde wept as though his heart had cracked. And it would have been the most soulless of men, hearing that bitter wailing, who was not moved by the utter desolation of the sound.

For Hyde had realized why the drugs were not working.

It was the *original* powders that were impure.

Some freak, uncharted element had given them their power. Some unknown essence that Jekyll would never again be able to reproduce.

And there was only one more of the original powders left.

Once more and once more only would Henry Jekyll be able to assume his own face.

And what of Hyde?

He had two choices.

He could skulk forever within the confines of his creator—a kind of living death. Or he could face the world and the gallows as the double murderer he was.

Either way, he was doomed.

* * *

The first thing the three men stumbled over when they entered the hall was the body of Mrs. Johnson.

She was just coming round. When she became conscious enough to recognize them, she clung to Poole, whimpering piteously.

"He's here," she wailed. "In the house."

"Who, Mrs. Johnson?" Utterson feared he knew but wanted to make sure.

"That fiend, Hyde. He broke the dining-room window." She nodded in the direction of the laboratory. "He's up there. With the master."

She began to sob loudly.

The three men looked at each other.

"I confess I hadn't bargained for this," said Utterson. "We'd better alert the police."

"No time," said Enfield, his army training coming to the fore. "Henry may still be alive. In danger. We must break in. Now."

"Then we'll need weapons. We can't face that madman unarmed."

"I took the precaution of bringing a gun," said Enfield, producing his service revolver from the folds of his overcoat.

Dr. Jekyll and Mr. Hyde

"There are some axes in the garden shed, sir," volunteered Poole. "And the master's shotgun is above the mantelpiece in the study."

"You get an axe, Poole. I'll take the shotgun," said Utterson. "Cartridges?"

"In the bureau, sir, top right-hand drawer."

Poole began to lead the weeping housekeeper towards the stairs.

"Leave her, for heaven's sake, man," snapped Enfield. "Get the axe. And hurry. There's no time to lose."

SEVENTEEN

Henry Jekyll sat scribbling furiously amid the chaos of his laboratory.

Time was short and he needed to make his confession.

In the absence of a priest he was writing to the one person in the world to whom, he felt, he owed an explanation. His fiancée, Mary Carew.

He had taken the final powder and he was uncertain how long the effect would last.

And so his pen flew over the paper as though there were no tomorrow. For—for Jekyll at least—tomorrow might never come.

He paused for a moment, searching for the perfect phrase with which to justify the unjustifiable.

And then his chance to explain was gone.

The hounds were at the door, drooling at the heels of a fox that had gone to earth and left itself no exit hole.

Enfield's voice rose above the clamor.

"Hyde. We know you're in there. Open the door or by heaven we'll break it down."

Jekyll rose unsteadily to his feet, his head starting to swim. He grasped the edge of the bench for support.

"Hyde?" This time it was Utterson. "Give up, man, you are outnumbered three to one. You cannot escape."

"I warn you, Hyde," interrupted Enfield. "We are armed. And we mean business."

Armed? Good grief. Did they mean to assassinate him in his own home?

Lights danced in front of Jekyll's eyes. He shook his

131

head to clear it and saw, with a rush of despair, that black hairs were erupting from the backs of his hands.

Time was running out.

He must let his pursuers in before the transformation was complete. Perhaps if he had a few moments to explain . . .

Poole was attacking the door with an ax. The heavy brass lock shuddered with each succeeding impact.

"Don't break it down," called Jekyll. "I'm coming."

But the change was overtaking him more rapidly than he had anticipated and the sound that emerged from between his chattering teeth came from Hyde's throat.

Hearing it, the three outside redoubled their efforts.

"Let me by," he heard Enfield shout. "I can shoot off the lock."

Jekyll flung himself against the door, attempting to hold it fast against the onslaught, while the dreadful tremors racked his body and mortal fear coursed through his shuddering limbs.

He was dying. Henry Jekyll was dying.

A sudden explosion splintered the lock, showering shards of metal into the room. A large sliver of wood lodged itself in Jekyll's wrist, piercing a vein and sending blood pumping down over his clawed hands. He tore it out with a snarl, anger replacing the fear that had until then terrorized him.

Jekyll could feel his soul receding with the growth of the rage. He slid down the door and curled himself into a fetal position, hiding his head in his hands, trying to hold himself together and crying out for a mercy that he knew in his heart of hearts was about to be denied him.

Death faced him fair and square. And in his last lucid moment he felt the utter emptiness of defeat.

Then Henry Jekyll faded into oblivion.

The writhing body came to rest as Edward Hyde.

And with the rebirth, spawned of the anger, came the spiteful determination to wreak what final havoc he could. They might kill him but Hyde was damned if he would go to hell alone.

He would take that swine Enfield with him, at least. Hate welled up in him and a resolve that the young cavalry officer would never live to comfort Mary Carew —never reap the fruits of his disloyalty to Jekyll.

Struggling to his feet, Hyde searched around for a weapon.

As the massive door smashed open, he tore a bottle of sulfuric acid from one of the cupboards and prepared to make his last stand.

EIGHTEEN

And that was how they found him when they burst into the room.

A wreck of a man, more animal than human, crouched in a corner brandishing a bottle of acid.

"Keep back," he screamed, foam flecking the corners of his mouth. "The first one who moves gets this in his face."

Enfield stepped forward and raised his revolver.

But it was not Enfield who fired the fatal shot.

As Hyde raised an arm to hurl the acid in the young man's eyes, Utterson pulled the trigger of the shotgun involuntarily, as he would have done had he been faced by a mad dog.

Both barrels discharged into Hyde's chest.

The impact lifted him off the ground and slammed him back against the wall.

The bottle of acid smashed to the floor where it began to eat its way through the linoleum.

It is said that no one believes in his own mortality.

Edward Hyde was no exception.

The look in his eyes as he slithered to the floor was one of blank astonishment.

He came to rest in a bloodied heap, regarding the hole in his chest in a detached, curious fashion as though it was some minor irritant for which he had failed to bargain.

Poole was the first to move.

Rushing to the wounded man, he grapsed him by the

shoulders and began to shake him as though determined to rid him of what little life he had left as quickly as possible.

"Where is he?" he shouted, furiously. "What have you done with Dr. Jekyll?"

Hyde looked up at the butler and his face creased in the semblance of a smile.

"Good old Poole," he gasped. "Ever loyal, eh?"

The soft tones of Henry Jekyll issued from the twisted lips like the voice of a ventriloquist emanating from the mouth of a dummy.

Poole let go the shoulders as though they were red hot.

"Dr. Jekyll?" he said doubtfully.

But Hyde merely turned his head painfully and addressed himself to the lawyer.

"John," He croaked, his voice failing. "No time to explain . . . the letter . . . the letter tells all . . ."

Poole stood up, ashen-faced.

"Heaven help us," he said, "if the man doesn't sound just like Dr. Jekyll."

"I am Jekyll," said Hyde.

And that was the last sound he ever uttered.

Unless you count the death rattle that issued from his throat as he gave up the ghost.

Utterson placed the shotgun on the bench and picked up the pieces of paper.

Quickly he scanned the contents, his face paling as he did so.

At last he laid the sheets aside.

"What does it say?" asked Enfield impatiently. "Is it a confession? Has he murdered Henry?"

"Yes," said Utterson, gazing with something like compassion at the bloodied corpse. "It is a confession

. . . of sorts . . . And yes, he has murdered Henry . . . in a way."

"Don't talk in riddles, Utterson. Either you murder someone or you don't."

"Where is he?" Poole wanted to know. "Where's the master."

But Utterson didn't answer. He merely picked up the letter and began to read.

My dearest Mary,

This is the last time I shall wear my own face. A terrible calamity has befallen me. I have tampered with things beyond my control and have been cruelly punished for it.

In my pride, I sought to set myself above the gods and conquer the equal and opposite elements of good and evil.

I have learned, too late, the folly of my assumptions. For evil has conquered me.

Dearest, when you know the truth, try not to judge me too harshly. I ask only that you believe that my motives were blameless and that initially I meant no harm . . . only good.

For I was successful beyond my wildest dreams. I proved Lanyon wrong. I separated good from evil—physically. Or rather, I separated evil from good. For it was evil that I created—pure evil—all the evil that hides in man—and in me.

I created Edward Hyde.

Part of myself.

The worst part.

And the strength of his wickedness was such that I was overpowered . . . and, yes, I must confess it, I gloried in him.

In his love of life, his fierce enjoyment of all things, he felt more strongly, more ecstatically than I had *ever* felt. His lack of conscience, his immorality, were alien to me . . . and infinitely seductive. Hyde introduced me to sensations that I had never before dared to explore. And what harm, I thought, what harm if no one was hurt?

But then he went too far—this evil that was me.

He *began* to hurt people.

And by that time, although I refused to admit it, even to myself, I had lost control over him.

I had concocted a drug to transform myself from one being to another, but Hyde was stronger than the potion—even though I was not. He came and went at will, behaved as he chose, and each time I came to myself it was to find that some new atrocity had been perpetrated in his name.

And now it has come to an end at last.

Hyde is a murderer.

He has been instrumental in the death of one of my oldest friends—Lanyon.

And the only means I have of remaining myself and shutting Hyde out are henceforth denied me. For the powders that were an essential element in my experiments were impure and I can obtain no more. Should Hyde's personality overtake me again, then I have no means of regaining my own identity . . .

Utterson stopped reading and looked up at his stunned companions.

"You mean Dr. Jekyll did all those terrible things?" said Poole. "He couldn't have. He didn't have it in him."

Utterson gave a wintry smile.

"Apparently he did," he said.

"My god . . . Look."

Enfield was pointing in the direction of the body.

A strange metamorphosis was taking place.

Before their startled gaze the flat nose began to lengthen and narrow. The hairline rolled up and back from the bushy eyebrows which shrank and lightened until they formed a fine arch over the eyes. And the eyes themselves, still open in death, paled from graveyard brown to the clear translucent blue of a mountain lake. And while the features softened, the proportions of the corpse altered also, until what lay before them was the athletic body of a young man in his prime.

Edward Hyde had disappeared.

And in his place lay the dead form of their good friend . . . Dr. Henry Jekyll.

"I wouldn't have believed it," gasped Poole, "if I hadn't seen it with my own eyes."

"Precisely," said Utterson . . . and ripped the letter into shreds.

"I say," protested Enfield. "That was Mary's."

"And what good would it do her, pray, to read it?"

"It might explain."

"Explain what? That the man she loved was a mass murderer? I feel it would be kinder to spare her such knowledge."

"Then what to you propose to do?"

"I propose to send Poole to fetch Chief Inspector Watson."

"And tell him what?"

"The truth. Give or take a few facts. That Edward Hyde has been holding Henry Jekyll captive. That Dr. Jekyll attempted to break free and was killed in the process."

"By Hyde?"

Utterson nodded.

"I fancy that will be the conclusion drawn."

"Then where shall we say Hyde is now?"

"Does it matter? We were too late to apprehend him and he has disappeared. He will never be found. The hunt for him will continue for several weeks and then be conveniently forgotten. He will not be the first murderer to have escaped justice . . . nor, I fear, the last."

"But don't you think Henry's story should be told . . . as a warning?"

"A warning? It only needs to get out that Henry got this far for every hare-brained crackpot in the country to start experimenting. Much better that they should never know."

"And Mary?"

"I leave Mary to you. She will be deeply hurt . . . but she is strong. She will recover . . . provided she has Henry's memory to comfort her. What she might not recover from is . . . the truth."

Enfield nodded glumly.

"I take your point," he said.

"We are agreed then?"

"Agreed."

"Poole?"

The butler looked down at the body of the master he had known, man and boy, for twenty-eight years. Tears stood in his eyes.

"He was always the same," he said. "Even as a child. Always curious. Always getting into hot water."

Utterson smiled.

"I remember," he said.

"But he was a good lad at heart, sir. He never meant anyone any harm."

He knelt and gently closed the staring eyes.

And as he stood up again, the storm clouds that had been scudding across the sky cleared. The wind dropped. And a sudden shaft of moonlight fell across the face of the corpse.

In repose it had assumed an almost childlike innocence, the lips tilted in a smile. As though Henry Jekyll were not really dead but merely asleep. And dreaming of the greatest experiment in the world.